A HERO'S HEART

A RESOLUTION RANCH NOVEL
(BOOK 2)

TESSA LAYNE

Shady Layne Media
www.tessalayne.com

MEET THE HEROES OF RESOLUTION RANCH

Inspired by the real work of Heroes & Horses... Chances are, someone you know, someone you *love* has served in the military. And chances are, they've struggled with re-entry into civilian life. The folks of Prairie are no different. With the biggest Army base in the country, Fort Riley, located in the heart of the Flint Hills, the war has come home to Prairie.

Join me as we finally discover Travis Kincaid's story and learn how he copes in the aftermath of a mission gone wrong. Meet Sterling, who never expected to return to Prairie after he left for West Point. Fall in love with Cash as he learns to trust himself again. Laugh with Jason and Braden as they meet and fall in love with the sassy ladies of Prairie. Same Flint Hills setting, same cast of friendly, funny, and heartwarming characters, same twists and surprises that will keep you up all night turning the pages.

A HERO'S HONOR – Travis Kincaid & Elaine Ryder
(On Sale Now)

A HERO'S HEART – Sterling Walker & Emma Sinclaire
(On Sale Now)

A HERO'S HAVEN – Cash Aiken & Kaycee Starr
(On Sale Feb 27th)

A HERO'S HOME – Jason Case & Millie Prescott
(Coming 2018)

A HERO'S HOPE – Braden McCall & Luci Cruz
(Coming 2018)

WELCOME TO PRAIRIE!

Where the cowboys are sexy as sin, the women are smart and sassy, and everyone gets their Happily Ever After!

Prairie is a fictional small town in the heart of the Flint Hills, Kansas – the original Wild West. Here, you'll meet the Sinclaire family, descended from French fur-trappers and residents of the area since the 1850s. You'll also meet the Hansens and the Graces, who've been ranching in the Flint Hills since right before the Civil War.

You'll also meet the heroes of Resolution Ranch, the men and women who've put their bodies on the line serving our country at home and abroad.

Prairie embodies the best of western small town life. It's a community where family, kindness, and respect are treasured. Where people pull together in times of trial, and yes... where the Cowboy Code of Honor is alive and well.

Every novel is a stand-alone book where the characters get their HEA, but you'll get to know a cast of secondary characters along the way.

Get on the waiting list for Prairie Devil and the rest of the Cowboys of the Flint Hills
tessalayne.com/newsletter

COMING IN APRIL 2018 – PRAIRIE DEVIL

He's the Devil she shouldn't want

Colton Kincaid has a chip on his shoulder. Thrown out of the house when he was seventeen by his brother, Travis, he scrapped his way to the top of the rodeo circuit riding broncs, and never looked back. Until a chance encounter with hometown good girl Lydia Grace leaves him questioning everything and wanting a shot at redemption.

She's the Angel he can never have

All Lydia Grace needs is one break. After having her concepts stolen by a famous shoe designer, she returns home to Prairie to start a boot company on her own. But when her break comes in the form of Colton Kincaid, Prairie's homegrown bad boy and rodeo star, she wonders if she's gotten more than she's bargained for.

They say be careful what you wish for
To get her boot company off the ground, Lydia makes Colton an offer too good to refuse, but he ups the ante. Will the bargain she strikes bring her everything she's dreamed of and more, or did she just make a deal with the devil?

For those who teach us to love fearlessly

&

*to the friends and family left behind by the 22 Veterans a Day
who take their own life.*

CHAPTER 1

A S FAR AS resting places went, this one didn't suck. And when it stopped raining, the view from Johnny McCaslin's final resting place overlooking the bay would be downright gorgeous. But that did nothing to alleviate the all-consuming ache in Sterling Walker's chest. Or the guilt that he could have done something more. Anything, to save his friend.

As if condemning him, a breeze kicked up, spraying an extra heavy gust of cold rain across his shoulders. In front of him, just under the shelter of the tent erected to cover the gravesite, little Sophie buried her head deeper into her mother's embrace.

How could Johnny do it? Leave the ladies he said he loved most behind? Sophie had been the apple of his eye. Or so he'd said. The spitting image of her mother's red curls only with Johnny's bright blue eyes. Eyes that when the last time Sterling saw them, had been cloudy and dull with pain.

The Officer in Charge grunted a command and Sterling's eyes snapped to the flag-draped coffin. It was time. Beside him, their other best friend, Jason Case rose to his feet, arm tight in a salute. As if pushing through mud, he stood too, bringing his hand to the edge of his cover. This wasn't happening. Couldn't be happening. The *crack* of the rifles cutting through the rain told him otherwise. They'd survived

Beast. *Crack.* They'd been part of the honor guard at Johnny and Macey's wedding at the West Point chapel fresh out of school. *Crack.* Together, they'd survived countless missions, covered some of the worst territories in the world. Injuries. Fallen friends. The lonely muted trumpet sounding Taps pulled him out of the movie reel of memories. Johnny'd survived everything but being a civilian. Grief closed his throat. He couldn't swallow. He couldn't breathe. He wanted to scream. He wanted to pound the coffin. Tear it to pieces. Hell, he wanted to cry, but he wouldn't dishonor Macey and Sophie with his tears. Not when they were standing so stoically in front of him. He swallowed the hot ache and breathed in slowly, dropping his hand as the last note faded into the wind.

He slid a glance right to Jason. A muscle ticked above his jaw as the honor guard snapped the flag taut and began the intricate, slow process of folding it. They sat. In the distance a seagull cried, a mournful wail slicing through the steady rain.

The OIC dropped to a knee in front of Macey. "On behalf of the President of the United States, the United States Army, and a grateful Nation, please accept this flag as a symbol of our appreciation for your loved one's honorable and faithful service."

Sophie leaned forward, placing a pudgy hand on the flag next to her mother's. How could Johnny have left them? Left his little girl to grow up fatherless. Leaving Macey to go it alone? Anger stabbed through his grief. He and Jason had already made a pact. They were the girl's godfathers, after all. They'd never abandon Sophie.

And then it was over. The small gathering began to disburse. Jason nudged him before making his way down the chairs. Macey turned to them, eyes tired. "Are you sure you won't come back to the house for dinner?"

"Jason flies back tonight, and we need to catch the four p.m. ferry."

She nodded, clearly disappointed. "I understand."

"We're only a phone call away if you need anything," Jason said, wrapping an arm around her. "And we'll always be here for Sophie. You know that, right?"

Sterling crouched. "Uncle Sterling loves you, honey bear. I'll skype you on Christmas, 'kay? You can show me what Santa brought."

She nodded solemnly and wrapped her arms around his neck. Grief washed over him. Johnny'd had everything and it hadn't been enough. And his death hadn't just ended one life, it had ended two others.

"I love you, sweetie pie. I'm only ever a phone call away." He kissed her soft cheek, damp from the rain. Standing, he pulled Macey into a hug. "That goes for you too. Whatever you need. Jason and I are here for you."

She nodded into his coat, covering a sniffle. Raising her head, she took a deep breath. "Thank you two for everything." Her face crumpled, and inside, Sterling's heart crumpled too. "I know it means a lot to Johnny that you came out. He loved the two of you."

"I know." Sterling swallowed hard. He'd save his mourning for a bottle of scotch in his hotel room.

Jason clapped him on the shoulder. "Ready?"

He nodded. There was nothing left to say.

The thirty-minute drive to the ferry terminal was silent but for the constant rhythm of the windshield wipers beating like a heart, a bitter reminder of their loss. As they pulled into line, Sterling turned to Jason. "I never thought Johnny'd become a statistic."

Jason let out a small laugh. "We're all statistics."

"But he had the package. He had the girl and the kid. Everything we were fighting for. He had a nice life after he got out. And he destroyed them."

"Did you have any idea?" Jason pulled the car forward onto the ferry.

"Me?" Sterling shook his head. "I knew he was tired. And he'd mentioned he and Macey were having a rough patch. That he felt like an ass for dragging her down. Said he felt like he was at loose ends. But I didn't think he was suicidal."

"Me either. I just talked to him right after Thanksgiving."

They made their way topside and found two seats by the windows. "Me too. He told me I should get out if I wasn't happy. That it wasn't worth being sad every day. Find what gives me peace."

"Damn. He told me the same thing. That I should quit the family business if I hated it so much."

Sterling's stomach pitched. "Do you think we missed something? Like he was trying to tell us he had no peace?"

"Fuck, I don't know. But I can say when I was at my lowest point at Walter Reed, I kept a lid on that shit."

"Why? I could tell you were low when I came to visit you."

Jason narrowed his eyes. "The last thing I wanted was a military shrink pumping me full of pills. I was already on enough meds from the surgery."

"But what kept you from doing it?"

"Honestly? The fact that they didn't allow sidearms in the hospital. You'd want to die too, if you lost everything I did."

"But your family…"

"My family likes dressing me up in suits and parading me around to their friends. The injured warrior, home for good.

The rest of the time, they want to pretend nothing ever happened." Jason reached into his coat and pulled out a flask.

Sterling accepted the offering and let the scotch burn down his throat. "You know what pisses me off the most? Why the hell didn't Johnny tell us? At least let us try and help him? I mean, *Jesus*. Who kills themselves two weeks before Christmas?"

"Would you?"

"Ask for help?" Sterling shrugged. "I don't know. I don't wanna find out. But I can tell you this much. Johnny is the reason why I'm never getting married. Look at Macey. She gave up everything for him, and he broke her. I've never seen her so devastated."

The mournful blast of the ferry interrupted them as the boat glided away from shore, slicing through the dark cold waters with purpose.

"She grew up in an Army family. She knew what she was getting into when she married him."

"Sure, at first. But he was out. He was supposed to be normal. She wanted more kids, man. She'd waited all those tours. Endured all that worry. And he comes home, and two years later – blammo." Sterling shook his head vehemently. "Hell, no. I'm not doing that to a woman."

Jason shrugged "But what if you fall in love?"

"Love is for the weak."

"Don't let Johnny hear you saying that."

Sterling looked skyward, raising the flask. "Hear that? I'm not following in your footsteps man." His throat grew tight again, and he swallowed it down with another hit of the scotch. "You shouldn't have left us. I'm never gonna do to a woman what you did to Macey." His side pocket began to vibrate. Phone calls could wait until later. Until tomorrow. Or next week. Or whenever the hell he felt like talking again.

"What's next for you?" Jason asked after a moment.

"Fuck if I know. I just signed my separation papers first of the month. Figured I'd pop in on my folks at Christmas. Last Christmas I was overseas, and then all hell broke loose."

"At least they didn't medically retire you."

"Bad enough. Transferring me to sit behind a desk all day, pushing paper. I'll never go on another mission again." He'd never forget the day his superiors came and told him he could no longer be a Ranger. Part of him died that day.

"I get it. Mom and Dad won't even let me get out in the vineyards anymore. They're so afraid. Or embarrassed. Mom refuses to look at my leg." Jason took the flask. "Come to California for a few days. It will do you some good. You can charm the pants off some local ladies. Go dancing. You've been cleared for dancing, right?"

Sterling scraped a hand over his face. Jason was only trying to be funny, but it still cut. "Yeah. Just not jumping out of planes."

"That makes two of us. Think about it? There's a bar 15 minutes down the road where they do line dancing on Thursday nights."

"In *Napa*?"

"I swear. My family can fawn all over you for a change. Give me some peace."

"I wouldn't want to be a burden."

Jason rolled his eyes and snorted. "You do remember I live on an estate? You can probably catch a seat on my flight. Or come for New Year's. Make a fresh start."

A fresh start would be nice. Maybe the change of scenery would do him some good. "I'll think about it."

★ ★ ★

SOMETHING BUZZED AGAINST his cheek. He slapped it away. *Damn mozzies.* It buzzed again. *How in the hell did a mosquito get into a plane twenty thousand feet in the air? He was next out, so it didn't matter. But that couldn't be a mosquito. There was a rhythm to the buzzing.*

And he wasn't in a plane. He was spread eagle across his hotel room bed with his phone buzzing into his face. It was dark now. The clock showed nine-thirty. And the inside of his mouth felt like a stable floor.

Fuck.

The phone buzzed again. Goddammit. Why couldn't everyone leave him alone? He punched the side button. "What?" he growled. But even to his own ears, he sounded more pathetic than fierce.

"Sterling?" the voice said, surprised.

"If your name's not Johnny or Jason I don't want to talk to you." He might have slurred some of his words.

"You okay, Sterling?" the voice asked sharply.

In the foggy recesses of his brain, a lone synapse fired. "Travis?"

"What the fuck, Sterling. Are you drunk?"

It was definitely Travis Kincaid. "If you're calling to rub my nose in the Army-Navy game, I really don't want to talk to you."

"You don't sound so good."

Grief swamped him again, and he rolled to his side, seeing the flag-covered casket float in front of him. "We buried Johnny this afternoon."

"Oh man."

Sterling was grateful for his silence. Because really, what could you say when one of the men you loved like your own flesh and blood was now six feet under in the cold hard ground? There were no words. Only hurt.

After a minute, Travis spoke again. "You wanna talk about it?"

"No. I need to get a fucking life."

"The timing may suck, but maybe I can help. I'm looking for a foreman."

"Not interested."

"Will you hear me out?"

Sterling sighed heavily, rubbing his head and trying to focus. It wasn't Travis's fault he was well on his way to oblivion. "You do realize I'm not a rancher?"

"You worked on enough ranches as a teenager, you could figure this out. And you're military. I want someone with a military background."

"What the hell for?"

"I don't know if you heard, but I've retired from law enforcement. Starting up the ranch again, renaming it Resolution Ranch. I want to help other vets."

That cut through his fog. "Hang on." He swung his legs over the side of the bed and reached for the water glass, downing the contents in one gulp. Giving himself a shake, he forced his eyes to focus. "Say more."

"We all go through the same things when we come home. We're still focused on the mission. We make everything a mission. We forget that we have a say in how we live our lives. Over the last six months I've been working with Hope Sinclaire gentling mustangs."

"Wait. Hope Sinclaire?" he was pretty sure the only female Sinclaire he knew was an elusive blonde named Emma.

"Used to be Hansen. Married Ben Sinclaire about a year ago. At any rate, working with the horses has helped me.

Totally changed everything. I just got married too. Thanksgiving."

"No kidding." Jesus. Was the whole world suddenly pairing off? Didn't these fools know what they were getting into?

"It's amazing how things can fall into place when your focus changes. When you find your purpose."

He could hear the conviction in Travis's voice. He hadn't felt conviction toward anything since he'd been removed from the Rangers. He'd been floating like a leaf and every time he thought he'd land, a gust came a long and blew him some more. "Why me?"

"You're smart. You're local – you know Prairie. You know the Flint Hills."

"Used to."

"They're still the same." Travis cleared his throat. "Your pictures still hang in the Trading Post, and people know and trust you here. And you're Army. I want the ranch to serve all branches of service. Cassidy Grace recommended you."

"No kidding." Cassie had gone straight into the service when he'd gone to West Point, but they'd all been in high school together.

Sterling scrubbed a hand over his face, giving himself a little shake. "I don't know, man. I always figured I'd left Prairie for good."

"I thought you Rangers were up for any kind of a challenge."

"Rangers lead the way." Sterling raised the glass he still held.

"So join me."

"No offense, but I want more in my life than mending fences and vaccinating cattle."

"You think ranching isn't going to be exciting enough?"

"It's better than pushing paper. But, yeah. I want something I can sink my teeth into."

"How 'bout gentling wild mustangs?"

Sterling sat up a little straighter. "What else?"

"Building something from the ground up? Having a say in creating something that helps people just like us?"

He liked that. If only he could have helped Johnny. Was this Johnny talking to him? Reaching across the grave and giving him a kick in the ass? He might as well say yes. What else was he going to do? Line dance with pretty girls in Napa? He could do that just as easily at the Trading Post. "Are you sure you want me?"

"Absolutely. I'm not considering anyone else."

Travis was one of those leaders you'd follow into the fray in a heartbeat, and it warmed Sterling that Travis wanted him. They'd only met a handful of times over the years, but he liked Travis. Respected him. In spite of their age difference, they'd forged a bond over their similar histories in the service. "If I said yes, what would that entail?"

"First off, a 650-mile pack trip to Santa Fe with me and a few others on newly gentled mustangs."

"New Mexico?" Excitement sparked to life inside him. "But it's the dead of winter."

"Sure as hell is."

"Why?"

"Test ourselves. And the horses. You in?"

"When do we leave?"

"January 1st."

CHAPTER 2

"I THINK WE'RE all set for tomorrow, don't you?" Travis looked down the table to him for confirmation.

Sterling nodded. "I don't have any more questions." He and Cash Aiken, one of Travis's SEAL buddies, sat at one end of a big farmhouse table. In between, were Hope Sinclaire and her brother, Axel Hansen, who'd come up from Oklahoma, Travis's new wife, Elaine, and her son Dax. "Axel will travel with us to Boise City, where Hope will relieve him."

"Unless Haley goes into labor," said Axel.

"Right." Travis nodded. "Unless Haley goes into labor."

Sterling caught an exchange of glances between Travis and Elaine.

Hope cleared her throat. "Ben and Gunnar will plan to meet us in Santa Fe with the trailers on January twenty-ninth unless we hear differently."

Axel lifted his glass. "I think it's time for a toast. To the new year and the new ranch."

Travis shot a glance at Elaine and she nodded. Sterling bit back a snort. Newlyweds. Everyone found it so cute. The little looks and glances. The soft touches. Endearing. But all he could think of was the grief etched into Macey's face. Did they know what they were in for, should something happen to the other? A pang for Johnny knifed through him. He should be here. With the living. Looking at his wife and child with that kind of affection.

"We have something to add to the toast," said Travis looking expectantly at his wife.

Elaine's cheeks turned the color of roses and she grinned from ear to ear. "We're having a baby."

In a flash, Hope was around the table, giving her a hug. Axel extended his hand to Travis. "Welcome to the club, man."

Travis beamed. Sterling had never seen the man look like that. Look so happy. He forced a smile. "Congratulations. When?"

"Late June, early July," said Elaine.

"There won't be enough time for us to get a new round of mustangs fully trained and trekked," said Travis, "so I'll be relying on you to lead the next pack trip. I can start it, but want to be home in plenty of time."

"Sure thing." He raised his glass. "Like Axel said, to new beginnings. New life."

"Hear, hear," echoed the group.

Axel stood. "Who's headed off to the Trading Post tonight?"

Travis wrapped an arm around Elaine. "We're staying in with Dax tonight. Playing board games if anyone wants to join us."

Sterling slid a glance at Cash. They'd only just met, but already he liked the man's no-nonsense demeanor. "None of that domestic stuff for me. Thought I'd take Cash down to the Trading Post. Show him how the landlubbers ring in the New Year."

"Haley and I will be down there with Gunnar for a little while. Play a round of pool before it gets crazy?"

"Sounds great. See you in a bit." He waved as Axel and

Hope took their leave.

"Don't stay out too late, and don't tie one on." Travis gave him a downright fatherly glance. "We're up at zero-dark-thirty and off by sunrise."

"Got it, boss. Everything's ready to go. I won't stay out too late." Sterling shrugged into his shearling and jammed his Stetson on his head. It had been years since he dressed in anything but BDU's. His feet still weren't used to his old shit kickers, itching for the comfort of his tight-laced army boots. But it was New Year's Eve and time to move on. Start fresh.

The last few weeks had been an awakening. Sleeping in his old room at his folks for more than a few nights, pulling out his old work gloves and his Stetson. He'd treated himself to new gloves, but the cowboy hat was in good shape, and he enjoyed wearing it. By the time they arrived back to the ranch from the trek, his foreman's trailer would be here. A temporary dwelling while they built permanent structures this spring.

"You ready for a night on the town?" He grinned across to Cash. "It'll be crowded, but everyone's safe."

Cash was in rough shape. He was already at the ranch when Sterling had arrived a week before Christmas. Travis had mentioned they'd served together and that Cash had worked as a bodyguard at one time. But it was obvious being in open spaces spooked the guy. Which made their impending pack-trip interesting, considering most of the six-hundred some odd mile trek would be out on the open range.

Cash shook his head. "Nah. I'm gonna turn in early."

"I understand. If you change your mind, give a holler."

It was only eight when Sterling reached the Trading Post, but already the place was hopping. Axel waived at him from a pool table, lifting a pitcher of beer. Sterling made his way through the crowd, stopping every few feet to talk to another person he recognized.

"McAllister, great to see you." Sterling wrapped his long-time friend in a hug. "How long has it been?"

"Too damned long," Mike grinned.

"Travis gave me some of your root beer. When you going into business? That stuff's the shit, man." He had to admit, he loved this part of being home. Connecting with the friends he hadn't seen in years. And it seemed like everyone was out tonight – the Cruzes, the McAllisters, the Hansens, the Castros. Even the Benoit twins. Only the Graces were missing from his old circle. "They're up in Chicago," explained Mike. "Carolina was supposed to get married about a week before Christmas. Her fiancé died the day before the wedding."

"Man, that sucks." He took a sip of his beer. "I'm telling you. That's why I'm never falling in love. Too much damned pain."

"No settling down for you? We're getting old, man," said Mike. "I'd settle down in a hot second with the right woman."

Is that what Johnny thought Macey was? The right woman? He'd married her then broken her heart. "But what happens when the shit hits the fan? When one of you goes off the rails. Or worse, dies?"

Mike shrugged. "The higher the mountain the harder the fall, I guess." He grinned over his beer. "But I always was a risk taker. On the front lines, while you were in the pocket dancing like a ballerina."

"Fuck you. Someone had to be QB. My face was the prettiest."

"Damn straight about that," added Tony Cruz, pounding him on the back. "I'm surprised you didn't come home with more scars."

The comment caught him by surprise and his body went tight. "They're there. But not where you can see them."

Tony's eyes grew flinty. "I know the feeling, man. All the shit you can't unsee. And you can't tell anyone about either."

"Quit cryin' in your beer you pussies," Mike chided. "It's New Year's Eve. Time to shed that shit. Move on. We lost a lot last year. All of us. Cassie and Travis are always talking about not letting our stories define us. Let's not have this last year define the next."

Prairie had been through a tough year surviving a killer tornado, and it seemed he wasn't the only one who wanted to shed the past. "I'll drink to that." Sterling raised his glass. "To kicking the shit out of the new year."

"There's the one that got away." Mike motioned to the dance floor.

He swung around and caught a flash of pale blonde on the far side of the room.

Emma Sinclaire.

Goldilocks. His high school rival. He'd recognize those long legs anywhere. And that perfect blonde hair swinging down her back. The color of sunshine. Her older brothers were dark, but she'd inherited her mother's coloring.

"I always thought you two would end up together," remarked Cody Hansen, home between rodeo stints.

"Yeah," nodded Mike. "You two bickered like an old married couple. I thought for sure you two had the secret hots for each other."

"Right?" said Cody, shooting Mike and Tony a knowing glance.

"No, way." Sterling burned behind his ears. "Emma Sinclaire was a pain in my ass. Yours, too."

"True," said Tony. "But I always thought she was hot."

Sterling stole another glance across the room. Emma stood bent over the jukebox, jeans cupping a perfect heart-shaped ass. She turned, laughing, and his breath stuck in his throat. Fucking gorgeous. All grown up with a wide smile and miles of luscious curves. Perfect for caressing. Or more.

"Put your tongue back in your mouth, Walker."

"See?" Mike crowed. "I knew he always had the hots for her."

Sterling turned away. "Not. Interested. Never was."

Cody snorted. "And that's why you made it clear to the rest of us she was off-limits. You'd have taken any one of us by the throat if we'd asked her out."

He couldn't deny it. He'd taken it upon himself to personally screen all her pursuers. Someone had to. Her brothers had been too caught up in saving their ranch to pay attention to her. He'd been doing her a favor. It wasn't his problem that not one of them measured up to his standards. It wasn't because he wanted her for himself.

"Sterling was too much of a player for her," said Tony.

"Tell me about it," said Mike. "Everyone wanted Sterling. You were the flame and all the girl moths couldn't stay away. I couldn't get a date in town if my life depended on it."

"And since Emma didn't want him, no one could have Emma," added Cody.

"You guys are full of shit," said Sterling, not liking how the back of his neck heated. "Maybe it's because you guys weren't good enough for her."

"Who died and made you her protector?" asked Tony. "Three brothers weren't enough for the job?"

"Emma and I had a special bond." He smirked at the memories. He'd delighted in baiting her. The way her face lit when she got her undies in a twist was irresistible. And she was so smart. Working to best her kept him on his toes.

"Now who's full of shit?" chortled Mike. "You made her life hell. Always teasing her in front of Nikki Pope. Rubbing it in her face when you beat her by one point in debate."

His stomach flopped. The way they put it, he sounded like a real asshole. "But it wasn't like that. It was just friendly competition."

"Was it?" Cody stared at him. "I still think she was the one that got away and you took it out on her."

Was Cody right? Antagonizing her might have been the best part of his day, but he'd never meant to be an asshole. A little finger of guilt snaked through him. Cody's assessment held the ring of truth and squared with what happened the last New Year's Eve he'd spent at the Trading Post. He'd thought about making a move that night, years ago. But by the end of the evening, she'd made it crystal clear how much she despised him, and he'd gone home disappointed.

A weight settled in his chest. Maybe that had been for the best. If Johnny's death had taught him anything, it was that you couldn't pull another person into your orbit without breaking them. And he'd never let that happen to Emma. Emma Sinclaire was pure gold. Regardless of their antagonism.

Cody's eyes lit mischievously. "Bet you a ten spot you can't get her to dance with you."

Sterling glanced back to the jukebox. She fucking glowed with vitality. With life. He wanted that. Just the tiniest piece of it to rub off on him. Fill the holes in his soul. Longing arced through him. God how he'd missed her. It had been brutal at first. But eventually the ache had gone away. To be replaced with missions and life lived hard on all fronts.

"I'll add to that." Tony slapped a twenty on the bar. "It's

now or never. Because if you don't make a move, I will."

Fuck that.

Deep inside him, an old competitive spirit sparked to life. A slow grin creased his face. He hadn't felt this good since before he was injured and forced to leave the Rangers. "Game on, motherfuckers. Time to watch a pro at work." Sterling cracked his knuckles. There was nothing he loved more than a challenge. Especially when it came in the form of a pretty woman. And extra especially when that woman was Emma Sinclaire. "Hold my beer. She'll be putty in my hands in no time."

CHAPTER 3

"I 'M SO GLAD you decided to come out, Em," gushed Luci Cruz. "I need a fellow wallflower."

Emma laughed. "You're the furthest thing from a wall-flower."

"Except on a night when it looks like there's an impromptu reunion taking place."

Emma scanned the crowded room, then turned back to the jukebox, pushing in a handful of quarters. "Sure looks that way. Why do you suppose everyone's out tonight?"

"I think everyone wants to kiss the year of the tornado goodbye."

"Could be." She scanned the selections. "What shall we play next?"

"I saw they added Uptown Funk. Let's start there. *Oooooh.*" Luci grabbed her shoulder. "Look look look."

Emma spun around, scanning the bar.

"Don't make it obvious," Luci hissed.

"Who is it?"

"Sterling sex-on-a-stick Walker. Looking mighty fine."

Groaning, Emma turned back to the jukebox, scanning for more songs. "Give me a break. I will happily live the rest of my life without seeing his face ever again."

Luci snorted. "Good luck. His face is plastered all over the wall of fame."

"Not looking."

"What happened between you two? I always got the feeling you liked him when we were younger."

"I liked his brain. Kept me on my toes. I didn't like *him*. Don't you remember how awful he was? He never lost an opportunity to humiliate me. I think he manufactured opportunities."

"Aww, he probably didn't know how to act around you."

She turned, narrowing her eyes at one of her oldest friends. "This is Sterling Walker we're talking about. He knew how to act around girls."

Luci giggled. "True that."

"I mean, really. Is there any girl in town he didn't kiss at least once?"

Two pink spots bloomed on Luci's face and a stab of jealously wound through Emma. She was literally the only person in town he'd never kissed. Sterling had put the moves on pretty much every other girl in town. She brushed aside the feeling. It was a long time ago. And Sterling was a player. He lived for the ladies and she'd lived for her studies. She'd been going places, then. Checking all the boxes on her list so she could attend the college of her dreams.

"You too, huh?"

Luci rolled her lips together. Gazing skyward, she gave a little shrug, face turning a deeper shade of pink. "I'm sorry I never told you. I didn't want you to be upset. It was only once, and I was sloppy drunk."

Shaking her head, she put up a hand. "I don't want to know. Really. And I never had a claim on him."

"Sometimes it seemed like you did."

Emma shook her head. "Nah. We just had this weird competition thing going. He was smart, but he was also a super jock. Mr. Popular. I was just book smart." She'd worked so hard to become Valedictorian, and in the end, she'd had to share that honor with him too.

"We were both cheerleaders."

Emma snorted. "We were *all* cheerleaders, Luci. That was Nikki Pope's domain and she ruled that squad with an iron fist." Unease balled in her belly. She hated rehashing her high school experience. Even with the success she'd garnered at Royal Fountain Media in Kansas City – the fancy loft, the name recognition, her picture on the society pages – every time she returned home to Prairie, she was still the awkward teenager with the hot older brothers, the philandering dad, and the socially awkward demeanor. It didn't matter that she'd been named to the *Thirty Under Thirty* list and that she was kicking around ways to start her own agency. In Prairie, she was plain 'ole Emma Sinclaire. Most of the time, she didn't mind it. She liked Prairie. Loved coming home to spend time with her family. And she was so much more now than who she was then. But seeing Sterling Walker brought all her old discomfort flooding back.

Luci tapped her. "Quick, quick, quick. Turn around. He's walking over here. Oh sweet Jesus, he looks fine." Luci clutched her arm, giggling. "And get ready, 'cause his eyes are on you, Em."

Emma zeroed in on the jukebox selections, but the words swam before her. All she could focus on was the flame heating her from the inside out. Her pulse quickened. Half in anger, half in anticipation. She hadn't seen him in years. What *should* she say? She sure as heck wasn't going to let him get the upper hand. Never again.

She turned at the tap on her shoulder, dimly aware that Luci had disappeared into the ether. She was entirely on her own with her nemesis. But her words died on her lips when she locked gazes with Sterling. His gray eyes glinted with humor and confidence. As if he already knew he'd won whatever match they were about to have.

The years had been good to him. Too good. No one should look as good as he did. Not without significant help from Photoshop. But there he was, standing before her, big and broad. Chiseled. Hard from years of service. Somehow his nose was still as straight as a Greek god's. And his mouth still had the faintest quirk at the corner, just the way it always had when they'd locked gazes. And his lower lip was just as enticing as ever. Begging to be sucked and tasted.

"Hello, Goldilocks."

His voice had matured too. Deep and gravelly. Like the aged scotch her brothers liked so much. He braced an arm against the wall with the air of a man supremely confident. She swallowed at the way his muscles pulled on his shirt.

"Care to dance?"

Something in the tone of his voice snapped her out of her trance. He was toying with her. She could tell. Everything about his body language screamed set-up. She scanned the room, looking for his cohorts, finding them leaning against the bar watching the exchange avidly. Of course. Mike McAllister, Cody Hansen, and Tony Cruz. The four had been inseparable in high school. Some things never changed. She looked at him coolly, raising an eyebrow. "You can tell your friends I was just leaving."

But that didn't put him off in the least. Instead, he turned his million-dollar smile on her and slid a hand down her arm. His caress burned through her sweater. She might have liked him once upon a time, but he'd never had *this* kind of an effect on her. The kind of effect that had her lady bits throbbing and her nipples puckering to tingly points.

"Just one? For old time's sake?"

"I didn't realize we had old times." It had suddenly become too warm in here.

His eyes crinkled at the corners. "Sure we did. You and Lydia Grace acting like librarians at the keggers."

"Someone had to make sure you boys didn't drink and drive."

"Stealing your clothes when we all went skinny-dipping in Kincaid's pond."

"That was you? I knew it." She glared at him. Of all the nerve. She'd had to tread water for what felt like hours until Carolina Grace had heard her shouting and had ridden home for a change of clothes.

He lifted his chin as a laugh rumbled through his chest. "The look on your face was priceless when we took off."

"I'm sure it was," she said dryly. "Thanks for the memory, Sterling."

"Aww." He drew his hand down her arm again, brushing to her fingertips. "You had your revenge when you got Cassidy Grace to steal my locker number and you filled it with slime."

In spite of herself, she laughed. "You deserved it."

He shrugged easily. Like he didn't have a care in the world. "Yeah, I did."

Huh. That was the closest she'd ever come to receiving an apology from him. Her resolve began to weaken. If she was going to escape his spell, she needed to plan an exit soon. And there was his mega-watt smile again. If he was trying to wear her down, he was succeeding.

"What do you say?" He extended his hand.

Would it be so bad? Dancing with him? Maybe he'd

changed. She had. The juke-box flipped to an old Kaycee Starr song, *Dance with Me.* One of her favorites. She would live to regret this, but she couldn't turn him down. She never could. "Just one dance."

He stepped close and took her hand. There was something so strong, so sure in his grasp. Electricity zipped up her arm setting her pulse hammering. She caught a glimpse of his buddies as he spun her into his arms and remembered to keep her distance. He was overpowering enough at arm's length. "How much they bet you?"

Sterling's eyes lit. "Thirty?"

"That all?"

He shrugged, a rueful grin playing at the corner of his mouth. "There was a chance you might say no."

"I almost did."

He tipped his head closer to hers. "Then I'll consider this my lucky day."

A shiver of attraction skittered down her spine as she caught his gaze and held it. His voice held a note of sin and promise. It would be so easy to give in. Become another in a long line of conquests. But, no. Not tonight. Not ever. She looked away.

His hand at her hip gave her a little squeeze, somehow acknowledging what had just passed between them. "I should thank you, you know."

She glanced up sharply. "How so?"

His eyes were sincere. He wasn't teasing her this time. "You made me work."

"What do you mean? Everything came easy to you."

"Some things easier than others," he admitted. "But I don't think I'd have gotten the appointment to West Point without pushing myself to beat you."

"The competition didn't hurt me either. I was ready for Barnard when I arrived."

"I wasn't."

"Ready for West Point? For real?" His admission shocked her. "The great Sterling Walker unprepared?"

He maneuvered them between two other couples. "No one is prepared for Beast. Not even me. But that's the point. It's supposed to be brutal. You're supposed to want to quit, but you don't. It builds you up."

Her respect for him went up a notch. "How'd you get through that?"

He studied her intently while the last notes of Kaycee Starr's song faded. Heat bloomed across her chest as the strains James Arthur's *Say You Won't Let Go* filled the bar. When he finally spoke, his voice came out with a burr. "You dig deep. Remember the people you love at home and why you're there. And the people you're letting down if you give up."

"There's no way you ever would have quit, Sterling. It's not your style." But still, she couldn't imagine what it must have been like, if he was admitting it was hard. Especially to her.

His expression turned serious. "Can I ask you something?"

Her heart began to thump erratically. "Sure?" Sterling was never serious. At least not with her. She tensed as she waited for him to speak.

"Do you think I'm an asshole?"

"Sorry?"

"Do you think I'm an asshole?"

He was serious too. She opened her mouth but no sound came out. How in the hell was she supposed to answer that?

His face tightened. "Your face says it all. You think I am. I *was*. Shit." He stopped in the middle of the dance floor, putting both his hands on her shoulders. "I was an asshole. To you for sure, and probably to others. And I have no excuse for my behavior except that I was a teenaged dumbshit. If I hurt you in any way I'm truly sorry. I never wanted to hurt you."

A rush of feeling flooded her, pricking her eyelids with hot tears. She would *not* cry in front of Sterling. "I... thank you," she finished lamely. What else could she say? She'd never admit to the countless soaked pillows, or the tears she'd cried into her horse's mane.

The song switched to Brad Paisley's *Then* as the clock crept toward midnight. Sterling pulled her back into his arms, and this time she let him pull her close. Maybe it was dangerous to do so, let herself get close enough to catch a whiff of his spicy cologne. He was so charming. It would be so easy to melt into him. Lose herself in a kiss or four.

"Emma?"

She tilted her face up, pulse rocketing. There was something urgent in his voice. Intense. "Yes?"

"Do you think we could start over?" His eyes were soft. Hopeful.

"What do you mean, start over?"

"You know. Be friends. I retired from the military and I'm home to help Travis with Resolution Ranch. I don't know how often you make it back to town, but you know, maybe we could grab a beer sometime. Catch up."

"Catch up." He'd stunned the speech right out of her. For a split second, she flashed to a previous New Year's Eve where Sterling had sweet-talked her into thinking he was interested in her. But she knew better. The road to hell was paved with good intentions. Just ask her mother about her father. She could move beyond the past, but she wasn't ready to get cozy with Sterling, no matter what her body screamed to the contrary. "Maybe." She smiled coyly. "So long as you never call me Goldilocks again."

"Aww." He shook his head, eyes crinkling again. "That might be a deal breaker. You can't take away all my fun."

Even she had to laugh with him. "Only most of it."

Ten, nine, eight... The crowd began to chant the final countdown to the new year. The room quivered with excitement. *Seven... six...*

Sterling tightened his embrace and leaned in. "How about it, Goldilocks? A New Year's kiss for old time's sake? To celebrate old friends becoming new?"

Five... Four

She trembled, flushing with heat. "Mmm. Tempting." She could taste him already. His eyes hooded, and for one heart-stopping second, she melted into him.

Three...

But this was Sterling the player.

Two...

Sterling the charmer.

One...

And if she wasn't very careful, she'd end up on the road to heartbreak. Just like her mother did with another charmer years ago.

Happy New Year!

She slid a hand over a rock-hard pec, resigning herself to an intense session with her vibrator. "But not tonight. Good night, Sterling."

She turned and left him standing in the middle of the dance floor before she could change her mind.

CHAPTER 4

Two weeks later

STERLING HUDDLED DEEPER into his coat, squinting into the snow flurries. They were going to have to break for the day if the visibility got any worse. Weather reports had called for blowing snow. He didn't realize that meant nearly whiteout conditions even though less than six inches covered the ground.

Axel pulled up next to him. "I'd give my left nut for a hot shower right now."

Sterling chuckled. "Suck it up. You'll have your shower tomorrow. We still have two weeks."

"I don't know how you guys do it."

"Easy. This ain't so bad." He'd loved every minute, so far. Sure, parts had been brutal. Slogging through ice had sucked. Unfreezing his hands hurt. Working to forge a connection with his horse, Bingo, and his pack horse, Trixie, was an ongoing challenge, but he was getting there. "For starters, no one's shooting at us."

"Hope's meeting me at our rendezvous point tonight."

No chance of breaking early, then. No problem. He was tired, but nowhere close to breaking. The weather would have to throw much worse at him before he'd throw in the towel. And if the horses could hack it, he could too.

Axel reached to pat his horse, Ricky, on the neck. "I want

you to focus on one thing with your mounts the last phase of this journey."

"What's that?"

"You're still treating your horse like an obstacle to over-come. That's why she gets tetchy. You're like a wolf hunting prey, and she picks up on that. You've gotta bring it down. Dial into Bingo's feelings, Bingo's anxiety. What makes her tick. If she's anxious, it's probably because she doesn't feel safe with you yet."

That stung. He liked Bingo. This was the most riding he'd done in years, and he'd forgotten how much he loved being out on horseback. The sore, achy muscles were worth it. But Axel was right. Every morning he went through the same ordeal with Bingo, struggling to settle her. Struggling to get her saddled, to clean her feet. Like he was starting all over with the horse again. It frustrated him that he couldn't wrap his head around that part of it.

"I don't get it. I don't know what I'm doing wrong."

Axel shrugged. "It's hard to say. On the outside, you're doing all the right things."

"So it's me," he said, trying not to let disappointment creep into his voice. "You're saying she has a problem with *me*."

"You'll probably hear Hope say this when she joins y'all. A horse can sense your bullshit long before you do. They won't trust you unless you're completely honest with them. Or yourself."

Huh. Sterling blew out a breath. "So you're saying I haven't been honest with the horse?"

That sounded far-fetched. But Bingo was right.

He'd wrapped himself in a cloak of supreme confidence for the sake of the mission for so many years, he wasn't sure it could come off. It was baked into his skin, like an exoskeleton. Was that what Emma had reacted to for so many years? She'd grown up around horses, so it was possible. It was also possible she had a sensitive bullshit meter.

Was that why she'd fled on New Year's Eve? Her bullshit meter had gone haywire? For a shining, sweet moment, he'd felt a connection with her. Something true and deep. He'd never have suggested a kiss otherwise. He was a risk-taker, not a glutton for punishment. But he'd fallen back on his favorite *MO* – his irresistible charm.

Still, she hadn't said no.

He'd take *not tonight*. Those words held a glimmer of hope. She could have told him to fuck off. He'd half expected her to, so he'd count *not tonight* as a win.

Grief stabbed through him as Johnny's laugh rang through his head. *Someday, Walker... You're not going to know what hit you. And I'll be laughing my ass off when the woman of your dreams conks you on the head with a two-by-four.*

He swallowed against the tightness in his throat. Nope. There would be no woman of his dreams. Not if he couldn't guarantee her happiness. And nobody could do that. Not even Superman.

He tossed and turned that night, tent flapping in the wind. A rock dug into the small of his back. Cold seemed to permeate his sleeping bag. His dreams were haunted by faces. Jason's grimace of agony at Walter Reed. Johnny's vacant hopeless stare the last time they'd shared a meal. Macey's face pinched with grief. Emma's sparkling eyes on New Year's Eve, her smile reflecting all the light in the room. He woke grouchy and bone tired. His knee ached.

The tent rattled.

"Up and at 'em. We're burnin' daylight," Hope's voice

called from the other side.

He dressed quickly, hands stiff from the days of holding reins and pack-lines. A fire crackled in the crisp air and the few remaining clouds fired in shades of orange and coral. It was quite a vision, three-hundred-sixty degrees of white expanse, hardly a tree in sight. Today would be a long ride. They'd finish in the dark, passing through the Rita Blanca National Grasslands and making camp somewhere outside of Clayton New Mexico. This part of the United States was as desolate as any place he'd been in the Sandbox. He appreciated the stark beauty of it. The myriad of stars by night, and the vast emptiness by day that reminded him of his insignificance. Demanded his respect.

Hope handed him a steaming cup of coffee. He wrapped his hands around the camp mug, drawing warmth from the sides.

"Axe mentioned you've been having trouble with Bingo?"

"It's nothing. She's just ornery."

"I trained Bingo. She's not ornery. But she is particular. And mistrustful." She eyed him critically. "How much time do you spend with her not riding?"

"None." He shifted uncomfortably. He'd been too busy helping make camp or taking his turn at meal prep. Besides, Bingo was just a horse.

"Finish up your coffee and go spend ten minutes with her. Don't touch her. And don't look her directly in the eye. That's a predatory move. Just stand there. Be with her. Get your breathing in sync with hers. And then talk to her. Can be about anything you want. Keep your voice soft and low. I'll come check on you when you're done.

"That's it? You want me to talk to my horse?"

Hope flashed him a grin. "Or you could continue with

your current struggle." She shrugged. "Up to you."

Johnny was surely laughing down at him now.

He gulped down his coffee and jammed his hands deep into his coat pockets, making his way to where the horses were corralled. Bingo stood on the end, next to Trixie. She swung her head his direction as she heard him approach. He stopped a little more than an arm's length away. Her tail flicked, and she turned her head away, pawing the ground. Same as every morning. But this time he stood there, studying her, trying to sync his breathing to hers.

After a minute or two, he caught it. All at once, his belly warmed. His awareness expanded. In the distance a songbird chirped. Behind him, he could hear the camp noises as Cash prepared breakfast. The smell of sausage drifted over. This was different than the adrenaline driven hyperawareness of a mission. This was... softer. Scarier.

It hit him. He wasn't in control. Fear and excitement pressed on his chest, squeezing his throat. He'd never felt so vulnerable... so exposed. After a minute she turned her head back toward him again. Like Bingo was looking right into his soul.

"Hey, girl." The words rose unbidden. "Did you rest okay? Ready for a big day?" He took a shuddering breath. "I didn't sleep so well."

It felt so strange. Talking to a horse like little Sophie talked to her stuffed animals. But if she could do it, so could he.

He started again. "So... I have a friend who died." The air in his chest squeezed out. "I really miss him, and I'm having trouble figuring out my life. I'll tell you, because you're a horse and you're not going to say anything, but I think I'm doing a piss-poor job of it right now. And I want to help other guys like us. And I don't know how. And I'm cold and tired, and we still have two weeks left on this crazy Santa Fe Trail trek, and I can't stop thinking about Emma."

CHAPTER 5

Early February

EMMA TURNED ONTO the long drive of the Kincaid ranch. Resolution Ranch would take some getting used to, but she liked it. Liked the ring of it, and the images it conjured. She'd worked hard the last month, sketching ideas, floating possibilities to some of her best clients. She'd spent more late nights on this project than all her others combined. Prairie needed this ranch to be successful as much as Travis did.

She settled a nervous flutter in her belly. Travis would be the first person in Prairie to see her work. Her brothers admired her success, but they weren't interested in the details. They were just happy to see her when she came home.

If Travis liked her ideas, it would give her the confidence to approach some of the other businesses in town. Maybe even start a mini business incubator as part of her help with the reconstruction efforts. There were so many talented people in Prairie who just needed a little help getting their businesses noticed. She might not be good at ranching, or teaching school, or running a diner, but she was great at bringing attention to people and causes.

She came over the rise and hit the brakes, gasping at the beauty before her. It had been years since she'd been on the Kincaid property. She'd forgotten how sweet it was. The main house and barn stood nestled between two gently sloping hills dotted with trees. A new coat of red paint on the barn screamed Americana. The perfect image for a ranch committed to helping veterans, and the donors would fall in love with it. She'd have to return later in the month with a photographer and videographer to grab some good promo pictures for her print work and social media. And again, when the prairie bloomed later in the spring. She wouldn't change a thing.

Except maybe for Sterling's presence. The nervous flutter in her belly grew to a full-fledged two-step. He'd surprised her New Year's Eve, and she'd replayed their conversation over and over. Had he really changed? Or was he yanking her chain the way he always did?

Does a leopard change its spots?

She would have to do her best to resist him when he turned on the charm. She'd come entirely too close to kissing him New Year's Eve. Her lips still tingled at the thought of it. But if this ranch was like her family's, she might not see him at all. They were most likely out checking fences and doing a myriad of other things necessary to keep the ranch running smoothly. She could be in and out with Travis and back on her way without Sterling being the wiser. And that would be for the best.

Grabbing her laptop and portfolio, she practically skipped up the porch to knock at the door. She was met by a woman who looked strangely familiar. Emma racked her brain. Normally, she never forgot a face. The woman was a few years younger than her, so they didn't know each other from school. And she didn't have the coloring of a Hansen or a Grace. Maybe 4-H? Perhaps they'd met at the county fair the year she was Miss Rodeo Princess. "Do I know you?"

The woman's eyes grew wide and fearful and she shook

her head vehemently.

Huh. Not the reaction she was expecting. "Are you all right? I'm looking for Travis."

She nodded solemnly. And stepped aside, motioning for her to enter.

"I'm Emma. Travis is expecting me?"

She was an odd bird, not talking, and just staring. "Are you sure you're okay?"

The woman nodded and pointed to her throat, giving a helpless shrug.

"Do you have laryngitis?" Emma swallowed, a sympathetic ache rising in her own throat.

Nodding, the woman scurried to the table and scrawled on a notepad. She ripped off a piece of paper, slapping it on the table, and continued to scribble furiously on the next page. Emma followed her and grabbed the first page.

They tried to reach you, but no phone... Emma glanced at her phone. Damn. There was a voicemail. The call must have come in when she'd been driving through one of the no-service areas. Lord knew, there were plenty outside of Prairie.

She handed Emma the second piece of paper.

He's with the foreman. They're running late. There's a fence broken in the north pasture.

I'm Kate.

She looked up. "Nice to meet you, Kate. I feel like we've met before. You're not from Prairie, are you?"

Kate shook her head.

"Well, I hope you feel better soon. Do you mind if I do some work while I wait?"

Kate gestured to the table.

Emma set her portfolio on the table and pulled out her laptop. With the resources she had at her fingertips at Royal

Fountain Media, she could put something extraordinary together for Travis. Even garner the ranch national attention, which is what it needed. Veteran's issues affected every community in the country. Prairie was a prime example. The VFW was as crowded as the Trading Post on any Thursday night. She lost herself in the magic of her ideas, fingers flying across the keyboard.

The door swung open on a gust of wind and Travis blew in, a blast of cold air swirling into the room. Another man was with him. Tall, bearded, and broad. "*Sterling?*" Her voice squeaked at the end. She couldn't help it. She barely recognized the ruggedly handsome man in front of her. He looked... hot.

He grinned, teeth glowing white against the dark scruff of his beard. "Nice to see you too, Goldilocks."

She couldn't get over it. There was something *different* about him. And it was more than the beard. She didn't normally go for facial hair, but she had to admit, he wore a beard like a champ.

Travis removed his jacket and came to the fireplace, stretching out his hands. "We hired Sterling to be our foreman. With my Navy connections and his Army connections, we should have a pipeline of folks we can bring on in the coming months."

"Fantastic," she murmured, rapidly rearranging both her campaign and her schedule. She'd planned to spend significant time at the ranch getting to know the staff and finalizing her promotional plans. She should rethink that. Maybe she needed to have another colleague take over the fundraiser. That might be the best thing for the ranch.

Sterling joined Travis in front of the fireplace. Emma dug into her portfolio, avoiding his sharp gaze. She'd have to sneak another peek at him when he wasn't staring at her.

"I see you've met Kate." Travis motioned to the young woman shrugging into her coat. "Elaine hired her while we were on the pack trip. She'll be helping with the horses. Cash is our only other ranch hand at the moment. He's putting up the horses, but we hope to have a full crew by the end of the summer."

"That sounds great. I know this is going to be a huge success." Emma swiveled her laptop around. "Would you like to see what I've worked up so far?"

Travis looked to Sterling, then back at her. "Actually, I'm going to stay pretty hands off this project. We're obviously looking to raise as much capital as possible by summer. And we're rolling out in phases, so even if we don't raise much our first year, we've got contingency plans in place to stay operational." He rubbed his hands together vigorously. "But as you know, Sterling's pretty gifted with numbers and logistics. Since we won't have much of a crew for him to manage until the outbuildings are constructed and the cow-calf pairs are purchased, I figured he could be your point man on this project. That would free me up to be the spokesperson for the ranch and not get mired down in the details."

Her stomach pitched. At the same time she fumed. This had Sterling's fingerprints all over it. He must have been trying to butter her up New Year's Eve, knowing Travis had asked for her help.

So. Typical.

She shot a glance his direction, pushing down the wave of hurt that swept through her. Sure enough. He looked as smug as a cat in front of an empty bowl of cream. He raised his eyebrows, gray eyes twinkling. He had no business looking so damned rakish when he was pulling the rug out from under her. "To be clear." She directed her question to Travis. "You want me to run all the details by Sterling?"

Travis nodded. "Everything."

"That okay, Goldilocks?" he had the audacity to wink at her. "I assured Travis we'll get along just fine."

The nerve of him. She should walk away right now. Hand the project to a colleague. She'd had enough of Sterling's shenanigans to last a lifetime. But something in his eyes prodded at her. He expected her to fold. She straightened her spine, keeping her eyes lasered on his. She wouldn't let him beat her again. Or show her up. She'd promised herself that years ago. He might be Prairie's Golden Boy, but she was at the top of her game. On the fast-track to becoming the youngest VP in the history of Royal Fountain Media. No way was Sterling going to jeopardize that.

She shot him a saccharine sweet smile. "So long as you stop calling me Goldilocks."

"We already discussed that, sweetheart. No can do."

Just ignore him. Don't take the bait.

She turned to Travis and forced her face to relax. "I'm happy to work with Sterling. I want this fundraiser to be everything you've dreamed of and then some."

Travis shrugged into his shearling and jammed on his Stetson. "Great. I really appreciate you jumping in to help us, Em. Cash and I are going to see to repairing one of the water pumps, so I'll leave you two to it."

Emma stood, glaring at Sterling as the door snicked shut. "Is this your idea of a joke? Because if so, you've gone too far."

CHAPTER 6

A SHOT OF awareness ricocheted through Sterling. How could he resist teasing her when she looked so spectacular all riled up and fierce like a prairie chicken? His breath caught. She exuded vitality, bright eyes snapping as color flooded her cheeks.

"No joke, sweetheart. Just the best choice for the ranch." And him, too. He couldn't deny it. She drew him like a moth to flame. She always had. "Travis doesn't really have a head for numbers and budgets. That's more his wife's realm."

"Then why didn't you suggest I work with her?"

She had a point. But the idea had sounded brilliant when he'd suggested he become point man. He probably wouldn't have offered except that Travis had mentioned Emma was leading their fundraising efforts. He flat out couldn't resist the opportunity to spend more time around her. Maybe needle her and challenge her, but only enough to see the spark in her eyes. To be honest, he'd missed it. He'd never met anyone who revved him up like she had.

He shrugged. "She's got her hands full with Dax and community college. And she's expecting a baby this summer."

Her eyes widened at that little tidbit. "Really?" It was sweet, the excitement in her voice.

He opened his arms. "Seems like you're stuck with me. Hope I'm pretty enough company for you."

She narrowed her eyes at him. "If you think this is an opportunity to steamroll me, you're quite mistaken."

A laugh rumbled out of him and he grinned at her. "Calm down. No one's going to steamroll you." Although he couldn't promise no pushback. It was too damned fun setting her off.

She stared hard at him, as if weighing his words carefully. "Fine. Do you want to see what I've put together?"

"How about over a bottle of wine at Gino's tonight? Do a little planning, then catch up?" Give him an inch, he'd press for a mile.

Something in the tilt of her head conveyed uncertainty. And for a split second, his hopes rose. But she shook her head. "Sorry. I have plans back in Kansas City."

Disappointment flashed through him followed by a jealous surge as he imagined her having dinner with someone else. He gave himself a mental shake. He had no business feeling jealous. Being out on the trail had reaffirmed his decision to stay away from emotional entanglements. He might be doing okay now, but if something were to happen… if he ended up like Johnny… Nope. He'd never bring a woman into his orbit.

But still.

Emma was different. They had a long history. And it wouldn't be right to pass up an opportunity talk with her. Engage in a little verbal sparring. Or more. His eyes raked over her. She looked so fresh and sweet, blonde hair pulled back in a low ponytail, jeans hugging her curves in all the right places. Mouth plump and begging to be kissed. His throat went dry as awareness zinged through him. "I'll take a raincheck then. When are you in town next?"

She eyed him suspiciously. "Why not now?"

It wasn't Gino's, but he'd take what he could get. He flashed her his most charming grin. "Sure thing, Goldilocks. Can I get you a cup of coffee?" He left the warmth of the fireplace and headed around the couch to the kitchen.

She tried to hide it, but he caught the roll of her eyes and the way her mouth quirked as she turned to her laptop. As if she was trying not to smile. "Fine. With cream, no sugar."

He reached for two mugs. "Too sweet for sugar?"

This time she giggled. The music of it lit something deep inside him and triggered a cascade of awareness skittering down his chest. He would definitely have to make her giggle again.

She met his eyes over the coffee pot. The snap in her gaze was back. And the pink on her cheeks. "Sugar is for sissies."

"That so?" Raising his eyebrows, he dumped half the sugar bowl into his cup.

Her eyes turned to saucers and she bit her lip, body shaking.

He gave his cup a stir, and took a sip, forcing it down without a grimace. Jesus, it was awful. He preferred his coffee black. This tasted like syrup. "So you saying I'm a sissy?"

She shook her head accepting the steaming mug, made just as she'd asked. "Sit down. I don't have all day." The note of laughter in her voice belied her brusqueness. Another score for him.

He sat next to her, draping an arm over the back of her chair. Her perfume mingled with the aroma of the coffee. A golden curl fell forward to her chin and he itched to return it to its proper spot behind her delicate ear. A vision of him fisting her hair and tugging on her ponytail ripped through him. Maybe Cody was right, she would always be the one who got away. The one who wormed her way under his skin and into his thoughts at every turn. Forcing his eyes away, he took another sip of his disgusting coffee and focused on her screen.

The plan was good… except. "No." He shook his head.

"What do you mean, no?"

"I mean no." He gestured to her screen. "This is all wrong."

She scowled, looking hurt. "How so?"

"You can't do the fundraiser in Kansas City. And I refuse to let you parade our guys around like a bunch of poodles so your rich clients can pat themselves on the back and feel good about themselves." He rocked back in the chair, crossing his arms emphatically. "No."

"And how exactly were you planning on raising money for the ranch Superboy?" she sputtered.

Her tone of voice implied irritation, but her face had become animated. Expectant, even. His cock stirred to life.

"Haven't given it much thought until today, but definitely not that way."

She swiveled to face him head-on. So close he could see the dark navy rim of her irises. "So you're steamrolling my ideas when you have none of your own?"

He leaned in. It would be so easy to kiss her. Close the remaining distance between them in an instant. "I'm not steamrolling you. But I am telling you this is the wrong approach. We're not a feel-good organization. This isn't a place for veterans to come and sit around a campfire and sing kumbaya. We're building a working ranch. This is a place for vets to rediscover their purpose and develop the skills necessary to lead healthy, productive, civilian lives. Your fundraiser should reflect that."

"I'm aware of that." She turned and snapped shut her laptop. "Tell you what, Sterling. When you have it all figured out, you call me and let me know." She pushed away from the table and stood, jamming her laptop into her bag. "Keep in mind this isn't something we can pull out of our asses. Not when I'm trying to help you raise half a million dollars. It's going to take time, and the right approach."

Shit. He hadn't meant to push her too far, but in his gut, he knew there was a better approach, and he'd fight for it. But he couldn't let her leave. Not like this. He stood too, and touched her shoulder. "Don't leave mad, Em, please? Why not take a look around? Have you ridden the property yet? Seen what we're really about and what Travis wants to do?"

The uncertainty returned to her eyes. As if she was conflicted about leaving. This he could handle. He raked his eyes slowly down her figure, dying a little at the way her chest rose and fell with each breath. "Of course if you aren't up for the challenge." He smirked and lifted a shoulder throwing down the bait he knew was her crack. She never could resist a challenge from him. "I understand."

Her spine straightened and the sparkle returned to her eyes. "I'm perfectly up for the challenge. Lead the way."

Before she could protest, he lifted her coat from behind her chair and held it open for her. His hand lingered for a split second at the back of her neck. At least she had the sense to let him be a gentleman. He might needle her, but he was determined to show her he was more than that. He reached the door first and opened it, gesturing to her. "After you sweetheart."

She covered a smile and glared at him, but not before he caught it.

But once inside the barn, she turned to him, eyes flashing again. "Where are the horses?"

He looked down the aisle. Shit. Kate must have turned

the remaining horses out to pasture. The only one left was Bingo. He couldn't help the smile that pulled up his mouth. He'd never look a gift horse in the mouth. Even when it was his. "Looks like Kate turned the others out to pasture. Sorry, Goldilocks, looks like you'll have to ride with me." He couldn't think of a better way to spend a chilly afternoon – riding the property with Emma snuggled up against him. His cock gave a little jerk.

The energy sparked off her. "I'm not going to double up with you." She shook her head firmly.

"Why not?" He leaned against a post. "Worried about the effect I might have on you?"

"Ha." She rolled her eyes again, but the quiver at the corner of her mouth was back, and her voice sounded breathless. "Not at all."

"Then you have no reason to say no…. unless you're…." He let the statement hang unfinished in the air. He had her now. He gave a mental fist pump, an answering thrill of energy ran through him.

"Sometimes I hate you."

"Nah." He shook his head, giving her a wink and resisting the urge to slide a thumb over her protruding lower lip. So plump, just begging to be tasted. But he wouldn't push his luck. He wanted to tease her, not get slapped. "You really love me. But you'll die before you'd admit it."

He led Bingo out of the stall, giving her a scratch behind the ears and talking to her like Emma wasn't behind him watching with a critical eye. He'd learned on the trip how to give Bingo his complete attention and to let everything else drop away. She'd sense any unease and stiffen up. For the moment it was only him and the horse.

He caught Emma's eye as he put on the saddle.

"You're good with her."

His chest puffed with warmth. High praise, coming from her. She'd been on horseback since before she could walk. "She's great," he said, giving Bingo a pat on the neck. "I've learned a lot from her in the last month." He took the reins and led her down the aisle and outside. "Hope is bringing a new crew of mustangs for us to gentle in another week. You should come watch. Then you'd have first-hand knowledge for your donors." And he'd get to see more of her. Just like old times.

After he'd double checked the cinch, he turned, offering his hand. "Ready?"

CHAPTER 7

R EADY FOR WHAT? There was so much meaning loaded into his word. The challenge in his eyes was clear. He expected her to bolt. She'd never give him the satisfaction. Sterling was right about one thing. She'd die before she admitted any attraction to him. He might be even more drop dead gorgeous than ever, muscles chiseled to hard perfection. The scruff he'd grown in the last month gave him a rakish air that set her core vibrating. But Sterling loved the chase. Lived for it, whether it was women or dreams. She'd not become a casualty of either.

But if Sterling didn't approve of her plans, she'd have to play his game. Treat him like one of her high maintenance clients. Soothe his ego enough to move ahead in the right direction. Travis had been a good friend to her family. Especially to her brother, Brodie. She was determined to raise as much money for Resolution Ranch as she could. And she wouldn't let Sterling stand in the way of what she knew in her heart was the best way to raise money for the ranch. He could show her around the ranch, and she'd adjust her proposal to include a few of his suggestions and whatever else made him feel good. But then she'd continue with what she knew would give the ranch the biggest visibility.

Her biggest concern at the moment was keeping her libido in check. His arm hooked around her waist, sliding inside her jacket, pulling her flush against his chest. A shiver rippled down her spine pulling her nipples tight. She handed over the reins, and his legs tightened around her as he signaled Bingo forward.

They settled into an easy silence, and lulled by the movement of the horse, she relaxed into him, his hard chest a welcome support. She breathed deeply, the clean air sharp and cold in her nose. A hawk circled lazily overhead, a stark contrast to the deep blue of the late winter sky.

"You like it out here, don't you?"

She liked how his chest rumbled against her back. And for the moment, she was grateful not to spar with him. "Mmmhmm. I'm not outside nearly as much as I like."

"Why not spend more time here?"

"Easier said than done. My job is pretty demanding."

"Of course," he murmured, his mouth above her ear. "I'd expect nothing less than that from you."

She swiveled her head and leaned back to catch his eye. "What's that supposed to mean?" She quickly straightened, heart pounding. The heat in his eyes had been too much.

"Nothing. Just that you always delivered everything with a degree of excellence that was hard to top. I can't imagine that's changed."

The admiration in his voice unsettled her. She could handle his teasing and goading. Gentle Sterling set her off-kilter. She cleared her throat. "So what goes here?"

"We're working on repairing the fencing and the water delivery, but the plan is to bring in longhorns."

Huh. While her brothers had broken the mold, and were on their way to developing the largest Bison herd in the region, most ranchers in the area ran Angus or Herefords. "Why longhorns?"

"First the novelty, but on deeper investigation, they're a heartier animal."

"My brothers switched to Bison for a similar reason."

"Longhorns are amazing. First, they just look cool. But they have natural resistance to a number of diseases and parasites. And they'll forage pretty much anything. For us, especially working with many who will be novices, it's a great choice. The cows are smaller, the calves are easier to birth. Shall I go on?"

"Sure. I'm impressed you've learned so much already." She liked hearing the excitement in his voice. It radiated off him and carried her along. In her mind's eye, she could see the pasture in spring, full of wildflowers and spotty longhorns. She had to make the fundraiser a success.

"They're easier to grass-finish, and your sister-in-law Jamey tells us there's a market for quality grass-fed beef. And since they have more live births and calve into their teens, it looks profitable for us. At least on paper. And it should allow us the funds to continue bringing in mustangs."

"Hope was telling me about that when I was home in January. I don't know who's more excited, you or her."

"I think we're all excited. Being a month out in the middle of nowhere with nothing but a horse and a few guys to rely on… changes you." His hand tightened around her. "I came home with focus. Purpose. I think we can make a go of this, and I want to give it my all. Anything to save someone like…" he took a shuddering breath. "A friend… I…" he stopped, voice thick with emotion, then shook his head. "I'm sorry. I can't."

Emma's heart squeezed into a painful knot. She hated hearing the pain in his voice. She wanted to ask more, but she didn't have the right. Not when most of the talking they did was sparring. She slid her hand along his arm, bringing it to rest over his.

She'd only ever seen him as invincible. Unassailable. Never thought of him as being capable of deeper feelings. But there was an unmistakable tone in someone's voice when they'd experienced deep loss. She'd joined that club too early in life. It made her sensitive to other people's loss. She squeezed his hand. "I'm sorry, Sterling. For your loss."

He squeezed her back in silent answer. He didn't have to talk. She knew what he meant. They continued over another rise and skirted the pond where they'd all skinny-dipped in as teenagers.

Sterling spoke again, the emotion gone from his voice. "So why'd you stay away from Prairie?"

"I could ask the same of you."

"That's easy. There were no opportunities for adventure in Prairie. You remember, my parents are educators, so I didn't grow up on a ranch. I wanted to be outside. Have an exciting life. See the world. West Point was a great opportunity."

"Then why'd you retire?"

He stiffened in the saddle. "Got injured in a training op and had to leave the Rangers. I'm only good for desk jobs now."

He said it with practiced ease, as if he didn't care. But Emma heard the note of bitter disappointment in his voice. "Are you okay now?"

"Yeah, thanks to a new ACL and months of rehab. But I'll always be an injury risk for the kinds of operations I want to be on. And at the end of the day, I guess I'm an all or nothing kind of guy. I made it into one of the most elite forces in the Army. Anything less than that was unacceptable. Better to cut my losses and start over. So when Travis called and offered me the foreman's job, I jumped at the chance. A new adventure, but at least I'll still be using my body and spending time outside."

The image of him as a warrior hovered in front of her. She didn't know the first thing about the military outside of the movies. But he was dreamy enough to star in a movie. *Her* movies at least. She squirmed as heat snaked up her legs, settling in her core. Just thinking about him in motion, using that magnificent body he'd spent years honing, set her pussy throbbing.

So much so, she missed his question. "Say again?"

"You avoided my question. Why'd you leave?"

"You'd leave too if you had three older brothers bossing you around and treating you with kid gloves. Besides, I was made for bigger things." His thumb really needed to stop caressing her rib cage. She couldn't concentrate on anything else.

"Like what?"

"Same as you. Adventure. Travel. My job has taken me all over the world. Every time I take a vacation, I go someplace new. But being based in Kansas City lets me pop over to Prairie to see my nephew and the rest of the crew."

"What's the craziest adventure you've ever taken?"

She laughed low. "You have to promise not to tell my brothers. They'd shit their pants."

His laugh shook them both. "Your secret's safe with me." He dipped his head and murmured into her ear. "I promise."

Her pulse hammered at her throat as tingles rippled down her neck. She was playing with fire, but something about telling him felt so right. She swallowed, her throat suddenly dry. "I spent three months traveling through Southeast Asia on my own."

"Impressive. What was your favorite part?"

Wait. Where was the shock? "That's it? You're not going to go all caveman?"

He chuckled. "Is that what you expected?"

"That's usually been the reaction. Some speech about how I shouldn't solo travel."

"My female colleagues in the Army would have strung me up by the balls if I'd ever hinted I didn't think they could handle themselves. Besides, I'm sure your brothers taught you all the moves necessary to stay safe. I would have."

Warmth spread across her chest at his admission. "They did. But I earned a black-belt in tae-kwan-do in college. He chuckled again. The sound toasted her insides like the hot whiskeys Jamey liked to make.

"No kidding? Remind me not to meet you in a dark alley."

"They don't know that either."

"The secret life of Emma Sinclaire."

She shrugged. "Something like that."

"What other secrets do you have, Goldilocks?"

She didn't miss the innuendo in his voice and it acted like an ice-bath. This was Sterling she was talking to. Her nemesis. The golden boy with flavor-of-the-week girlfriends. The one who was shameless about besting her at every turn. He couldn't be her confidant. "You've heard enough for one day," she said with regret. For a moment, things had felt... nice between them. And entirely too easy. If she wasn't careful, she could fall head over heels for this newer version of Sterling. "What's this?" she asked as she pointed to three trailers just on the other side of the rise from the main house.

"Temporary quarters. Those stakes and flags you see on

the ground mark where we'll be building a circle of tiny houses. Right now, we're thinking about ten. I'll have a larger house to the East that will also include the foreman's office. Once they're built, we'll be ready to roll."

The vision was truly impressive, and she had to admit, getting a personal view made her that much more excited about helping the ranch. As much as she hated to give him fodder for future shenanigans, she owed him her thanks. As the barn came into sight, she swallowed the tendril of doubt and spoke. "You were right. Seeing the ranch through your eyes has been a huge help. Thank you." The words burned on her mouth, but she was a professional. She'd always give credit where credit was due.

His arm tightened around her middle. "My pleasure."

"That woman, Kate. She looks so familiar. Don't we know her?"

"Nope."

"I'm sure of it. Are you sure she wasn't one of your weekly girlfriends?"

He made a scoffing noise in the back of his throat as he dismounted. "Always so quick to think the worst of me." He glanced up at her, eyes serious. "Truly. I've never seen her before in my life."

His hand was there to steady her as she dismounted. "Got it?"

It was sweet. Those little touches of chivalry. But not enough to make her feel helpless, or incapable. Just… nice. She turned, but he hadn't stepped back. Her stomach flip-flopped.

"I'm done with weekly girlfriends."

"I don't believe that for a second."

"I've changed Emma… Goldilocks."

The intensity of him, of his darkened gaze. The way his voice had gone rough at the edges. The sheer overwhelming mass of him, set her insides throbbing with anticipation. But it was the earnest tilt of his mouth that sent her pulse off to the races. He reached up and wrapped a strand of hair around his finger, caressing it as if it were a talisman. "I'm not the man I was."

Her mouth went dry. All she could hear was her pounding heart.

"Do you feel it too?" he murmured, continuing to twist her hair around his finger. His voice seeped into her pores. His gray eyes, molten. Hypnotic. She barely nodded, mouth parting slightly.

"Don't fight it. Let's not fight it."

"That's all I know how to do," she whispered.

"Break your date tonight."

"What date?"

Recognition flickered in his eyes. "The date you said you have tonight."

What on earth? Realization hit her. The 'plans' she'd referenced earlier. Damn. So. Busted.

"There's no date?" Something hot flashed in his eyes.

A shiver of attraction slithered down her spine even as her cheeks flamed. "No…. but I do have plans. For real."

His eyes grew flinty as he let out a low laugh. "Liar. You're just afraid you'll throw yourself at me, aren't you?"

So damned cocky. She socked him gently and stepped aside. "Keep telling yourself that." Thank heavens the spell was broken before she'd done something stupid like kiss him.

"I expect new fundraising ideas by tomorrow," he called after her as she made for her car.

"Goodbye Sterling."

CHAPTER 8

D AMN.

Damn, damn, damn.

He should have kissed her. He'd felt it. The pull. And she'd felt it too. She'd practically admitted it. But Macey's stricken face at the funeral had floated in front of him. Reminding him what was at stake. Holding him back. He wouldn't be responsible for putting a look like that on Emma's face.

At the same time, her mouth was too luscious to ignore. And the intense desire she stirred in him. Were his friends right? Was he taking his aversion to relationships too far? Emma Sinclaire presented a challenge too fantastic to ignore. He couldn't ignore her even if he tried. She'd been his drug from the time he'd first noticed her in seventh grade, stepping up to the baseball plate with the fiercest expression on her face, golden braids hanging down her back. He'd taunted her, daring her to swing at his fastball. *"Think you can hit it, Goldilocks?"*

"Bring it, hotshot." Her eyes had lit. As if she was going to enjoy putting him in his place. And she had. He'd underesti- mated her entirely. She'd hit the ball over the outfielder's heads, all the way to the back fence. Game on. He'd spent the next six years and then some, doing whatever he could to show her up, secretly admiring it when she beat him. When

he reached West Point, the space in his heart where she'd been transformed into a black hole. He'd never admit it, but he missed her with an intensity that took his breath away. Eventually, the hole closed and only a small ache remained. And by the time he graduated, the ache was nothing more than an occasional twinge. But watching her walk away just now, the ache returned with a vengeance.

What the hell was he supposed to do with that? If this was his idea of avoiding emotional entanglements, he was doing a shit job of it. But surely he could have a little fun with Emma and not go all in the way Johnny had? He wasn't looking for anything permanent. He was simply following the thread of chemistry spinning out between them. Shaking his head, he grabbed Bingo's reins and led her into the stable.

Cash walked out of the tack room. "We need one more for poker tonight. Want to join?"

He didn't usually play, but weekly poker was a ritual with many of the locals. He'd joined a couple of the circles when an extra was needed. But he didn't much feel like playing tonight. "What's the buy-in?"

"Fifty."

Usually his limit was twenty-five. "Who's hosting?"

"Sinclaires."

A slow grin spread across his face. "Count me in. What time?"

"Six?"

Perfect. Time enough for him to finish his to-do list and still clean up. "I'll meet you there."

Sterling parked in front of the enormous limestone house at five minutes to six. So this is where Emma grew up? He let out a low whistle. A far cry from his parents' modest craftsman in town. For a moment it felt like he was entering the lion's den, but he shook it off. The Sinclaires might be the oldest family in town, but they were still human. And he'd grown up hearing the stories of Wild Jake. Just like everyone in Prairie, the Sinclaires had endured their fair share of hard times. He stretched his arms over the steering wheel, cracking his knuckles. This felt more like meeting potential in-laws than a poker game, only worse. Brothers were always worse than parents.

"Just a friendly game. Nothing more," he muttered as he hopped out of his truck and took the porch steps by two.

A moment after he knocked, the door swung wide to reveal Emma's surprised face. "What are you doing here?"

This was too good to be true. Plans at home in Kansas City, huh? He was going to have fun with this. "Hello, Goldilocks," he practically crowed.

His elation crashed the second his eyes drifted to the blonde toddler in her arms. A kid? What in the hell? Disappointment pummeled him like a fist to the gut. It never occurred to him that she might have had a child. Something twisted deep inside of him and squeezed the air out of his chest. His face must have given away his shock, because she rolled her eyes. "This is Henry? My nephew? Who I told you about this afternoon?"

Of course. How had he missed that? It must have been one of those times he'd been staring at her mouth. He braced an arm against the doorjamb. "I knew that. Decide to stick around on the off-chance you'd see me?" He arched a brow.

Two bright spots of pink colored her cheekbones. "Look. I'm sorry. I really was supposed to head home tonight."

"So you stayed because you secretly can't resist me." He winked at her.

She snorted, but her eyes sparkled. "Keep telling yourself

that. You're nothing more than a player and I'm not interested."

"I'm not a player."

"Puhleeze. Maybe in a parallel universe. I was in every class with you in junior high and high school. I saw you at all the parties. I know how you operate." She shifted Henry from one hip to the other.

A vision of her holding her own child flashed before him. Again, something twisted deep inside of him. Something he was better off ignoring. "And how is that?"

"You love the chase. You can't stand it that someone might not fall at your feet and worship your hotness. And as soon as you've put another notch in your belt-loop–"

"Bed-post." She never could get her analogies right. "It's a notch on the bed-post."

She rolled her eyes. "Whatever. As soon as you've tallied your victory, you move on to your next target. No thanks."

"So you think I'm hot?" he goaded. A comment like that would light her up like a Christmas tree.

She groaned and shook her head, but it came out more like a strangled laugh, and he puffed up. He loved teasing her like that.

"I see you've met my boy." Blake Sinclaire joined them, taking Henry from Emma. "I'm hoping he'll grow up to be like you and lead the Mustangs to another state championship, and then go on to be an All-American."

"I'm sure he will, sir."

"Please. Call me Blake. I was long out of the house by the time you were in high school, but I'm not that old. Come on upstairs." He motioned Sterling into the house.

Sterling followed him through the great room and up the stairs, winking at Emma as he passed. "See you after the game?" He couldn't resist asking.

"Jamey will be up with snacks later," Emma called after them.

Six pairs of expectant eyes turned his way as he entered the attic. Cash and Travis leaned against an enormous pool table, beers in hand. Blake's brother Brodie, sat at the makeshift poker table, shuffling cards. Gunnar Hansen and Blake's other brother Ben, stood pouring beer from a tap behind a bar in the corner.

"Glad you could join us." Gunnar lifted a beer. "Want one?"

"You bet."

Ben handed him a glass of dark beer.

He took a sip. Holy smokes, it was good. Guinness-like, but with a note of vanilla. He'd developed a fondness for Guinness thanks to a fellow classmate from New York City. "What is this?"

"Tallgrass Brewing from Manhattan. Buffalo Sweat."

Figured the Sinclaires would keep a keg like that on hand. "Love it."

Brodie eyed him and began to deal cards. "Good. 'Cause that's all we've got."

An hour later, his jitters about the Sinclaire men had dissipated entirely. But he could tell where Emma got her sass from. Her brothers gave no quarter. In time, the table talk turned from animal husbandry to local gossip, landing on Army-Navy rivalries and Resolution Ranch.

Brodie piped up. "I want to know what he thinks of our sister."

All eyes turned to Sterling. He squirmed in his seat, heat racing up his spine. "Emma's a go-getter."

"And?" Brodie prodded.

Drop dead gorgeous, but he'd never admit that to any of her brothers. Not if he wanted to leave unscathed. He cast about for something safe to say that wouldn't offend her brothers. "And she's smart, too. She'd probably kick my ass at Monopoly."

Laughter raced around the table.

Brodie continued his grilling. "Travis said you're going to be point on this fundraiser. I think that's good. You always did give Emma a run for her money."

"And she always gave me a run for mine." Even during Beast. Every time he'd reached a low point, he'd ask himself if Emma would quit. He knew she wouldn't, so he'd pushed himself through. "She never quits. Never gives up. She'd have made a great soldier."

Brodie slapped his hand on the table, looking at his brothers. "Which is why she needs someone to challenge her. She's used to getting her own way."

"Sounds like someone else I know," Blake reprimanded wryly, giving Brodie a fatherly look.

"What you need, Brodie, is a good spanking." Brodie's wife, Jamey stood at the top of the stairs with a tray loaded with burgers. "Don't talk about your sister that way. There's a reason she's on track to be the youngest VP Royal Fountain has ever seen."

That caught Sterling's attention. "No kidding?" Add humble to her list of traits. It didn't surprise him at all that she was on the fast track to the top of her profession. He'd expect nothing less of her. But funny she hadn't mentioned it once.

Jamey turned to Brodie once she'd placed the burgers on the food table. "Emma's used to getting her own way because her ideas are brilliant." Then she turned to him. "Don't listen to my husband. What Emma needs is a partner. Not someone to boss her."

"I'll keep that in mind," he murmured.

Then it hit him. The perfect idea for the Resolution Ranch fundraiser. Something uniquely Prairie and sure to be a hit. He couldn't wait to share it with Emma.

CHAPTER 9

*H*ER HAMMOCK SWUNG *lazily over the sand, a sun-warmed breeze wafting over her, the sound of waves breaking in the distance. She stretched and opened her eyes as a shadow blocked out the sun. Sterling. "Come home."*

"You're blocking my sun."

He offered his hand.

Ding.

"Don't leave me."

What was that noise? It didn't belong on a beach. And neither did Sterling, dressed in his shearling and a Stetson.

She woke with a start. Heart racing. What in the hell was he doing in her dreams?

Her phone dinged again. Shaking the sleep from her brain, she glanced at the screen. Jeez. Was the man psychic?

S: *Where are you?*

She typed a fast reply, sleep pulling at her.

E: *Asleep.*

S: *I have an idea.*

E: *Let me guess. Does it involve sleep?*

S: *Are you inviting me over?*

She laughed, unable to stop a smile.

E: *No*

S: *Come over tomorrow and I'll tell you all about it?*

E: *Can't*

S: *Another mystery date?*

She deserved that. But she'd had every intention of driving home this afternoon, and then Maddie had begged her to work remotely one more day and stay for dinner. But after Sterling had shown up for the poker game, she'd tucked tail and run home. He was entirely too distracting.

E: *I'm back home in KC. Working in the office tomorrow.*

He didn't respond right away. And she shut her eyes, casting about for her beach dream. She could see the white sand. Sleep danced at the edges of her conscious. *Ding.*

Her eyes flew open and she stared at the ceiling counting to five before she looked at her phone.

S: *It's a really good one. Come out tomorrow?* ☺ ☺

She groaned and turned to her side. The man was incorrigible. Shameless. Adorable. And totally annoying. Her fingers flew.

E: *Let's get one thing straight. I don't ask how high when you say jump. I can come out again this weekend. We can talk then.*

A minute crept by. Then another, and another. She took a slow breath, letting sleep wash over her. *Ding.*

She sighed audibly and glanced at the phone, still in her hand.

S: *Okay. Looking forward to it.*

E: *See you then.*

She placed the phone on her nightstand, adjusted her pillow and shut her eyes, concentrating on slowing her breath. In her mind's eye, she conjured the beach imagining she could hear the crash of the waves.

The phone rang.

Would he give her no peace? She rolled over. "No. Not answering." The phone went silent. A minute later it rang again. She should turn off her notifications and stick her head under her pillow. But who was she kidding? Not only was her sleep shot for the rest of the night, but curiosity got the better of her. She rolled back over and grabbed the phone, punching the screen. "What?" she growled, now fully awake.

Sterling's voice came through the speaker like liquid sex. Hotter than a lounge singer. "Sorry to wake you."

"Your sincerity is overwhelming."

The phone rumbled with his low laugh. "I just had to tell you."

"And it couldn't wait, oh I don't know, until a normal hour?"

"Nope."

She could hear the unapologetic smile in his voice. Damn him for being so charming. "Lay it on me then."

"A high stakes poker tournament."

"WHAT?" She sat bolt up.

"Isn't that great? A high stakes poker tournament."

"You woke me up at two in the morning because you think we should have a poker tournament?"

"Mmmhmmm."

Of all the nerve. "Goodnight, Sterling."

"Sweet dreams, Emma."

It shouldn't send a thrill through her, the way he said sweet dreams. But it did.

And she had no business looking forward to seeing Sterling the rest of the week. But she did. The week moved agonizingly slowly, even though she put in fourteen-hour days. Her whole body seemed to relax as she pulled onto westbound I-70. The entire two-and-a-half-hour drive, she mulled over Sterling's crazy plan to include a poker tournament in a fundraiser. Whatever direction she went in, an initial fundraiser would set a precedent. It had to be big. Memorable. She wanted those donors to come back year after year, and if they weren't treated right, or her work was sloppy, they'd turn their backs. There were just too many opportunities to fund.

Her heart rate kicked up a notch as she pulled into Resolution Ranch. And it beat out of her chest as she trudged across the property to find Sterling working on building one of the tiny houses. His back was to her, and she took a moment to appreciate his physique. Sterling had always been built. And graceful. He'd thrown a football with the ease and elegance of Gene Kelly. He wielded the hammer he held with effortless grace, arm pulling the flannel tight across shoulders with every stroke. Even from several feet away, she could sense his focus. See how he concentrated with every cell in his body. And his backside. She offered a silent prayer of thanks to the universe for a backside as gorgeous as his. It was almost a pity to interrupt him.

She cleared her throat. "Lay it on me, Sterling."

He spun, lowering his hammer, heat flaring in his eyes as he raked a glance over her.

She gulped. "Your idea. Lay it on me."

A slow smile brightened his face. "High stakes poker. Everyone will love it."

"Just because you enjoy a friendly game of poker doesn't mean it's a good fundraiser."

"It's a great fundraiser." He laid down his hammer and came to stand in front of her. "And a place for your fancy donors to connect with the people they're helping."

"You said high stakes. What are you offering as a prize?"

"That's for you to figure out, sweetheart. Use all your fancy connections."

"Oh, no." She shook her head. "This is my baby and I am *not* letting you reduce me to a Girl Friday."

He stepped closer, jaw tight with impatience. Heat radiated from him, and she caught the fresh tang of hard work underneath his aftershave. "It's not your project. It's *our* project."

"Right. Just like our AP English project was our project."

"You did your part, I did mine."

"Bullshit. You stole my part. Took my idea and railroaded me."

"All I did was expand on your idea. Improve it."

"You stole it." All the old hurt she'd harbored came crashing back. It didn't matter how much time had passed, some memories reduced her to a teenager, with all the insecurities and hurts. "You couldn't stand that I might be better, or win anything."

"Our competition was good for us."

"Was it? It sure didn't feel that way when you stuffed the ballot box for Homecoming Queen. Everyone knew you and Queen Bee Nikki had a thing going." Even now, all these years later. Jealousy snaked through her, black and hot.

He had the audacity to look surprised. "I voted for you,"

he swore vehemently.

"Sure you did." Her body went taut, anger spiraling up through her belly. "And that's why you never lost an opportunity to make out with her."

His eyes grew wide. "What are you talking about?"

"Don't act so surprised. You think I didn't see? You looked right at me before you kissed her behind the home-coming float Sophomore year." She should let it go, but she couldn't. Not when he'd flirted so outrageously. Led her to believe he was interested, then kicked her in the stomach. "And then you *reconnected,*" she made air quotes, "the first Christmas we were all legal at the Trading Post." Ensuring she stayed far away from there whenever she came home.

He looked confused. If the memory wasn't so painful, she might laugh. She shook her head in dismay. "You don't even remember, do you? We talked most of the evening and I thought you were finally ready to let the old competition die. But you were just toying with me like you always do."

How could he just stand there looking like she'd sprouted a second head? Was he really so clueless? Or self-absorbed? What a fool. She'd been a fool. She held up her hands. "Look. Forget it." Defeat washed over her. "I'll figure out how to add poker. But I'm not driving back here again. I'll send you what I come up with."

She spun away, heading back the way she'd come.

"Wait." Sterling caught her arm. "I have no idea what you're talking about. The only person I wanted to make out with that night was you."

She turned back. "I don't believe that for a second."

"It's true. But then you left in a huff and I couldn't figure out why."

"Because you were kissing another girl," she yelled, giving

into the anger and hurt turning her inside out. "She asked if I was interested in you. Said you wanted to know. And stupidly, I told her yes. And when I came back with punch you were making out with her."

Understanding dawned on his face. "Wait. You like me?"

"Past tense, Superboy." She'd gone home and cried into her pillow that night, vowing to never shed a tear over Sterling Walker again.

He raked a hand over his head. "She said that Parker Hansen truth or dared her to kiss me and would I cooperate? That was all."

That sounded like vintage Nikki. But no. She wasn't letting him off the hook. Not when they were finally airing their grievances. "And you believed her?"

"Wouldn't you?"

"*NO.* It's Nikki Pope. How many times did you hook up with her in high school?"

"It was never like that. We were…. We were…"

"Friends with benefits," she finished, a bitter taste in her mouth. Ugh. Why was she pouring salt on old wounds? Because she wanted to hold onto her hurt. It was easier than accepting she'd left the Trading Post that night because she was too afraid to confront him. Too afraid to show her cards. And the fact that he did things to her insides all these years later – made her laugh with his corny flirting and drool when he handled a hammer, deeply unsettled her.

She took a stuttering breath and pinched the bridge of her nose. "It doesn't matter anyway. It's all in the past. But you never should have kissed her if you intended to kiss me."

"A mistake I won't be making again." His other hand came up to cup her neck and he dipped his head. When his mouth took hers, it was soft. Tender. Seductive. Not at all what she had expected. And it acted like fire in her veins, shooting through her in a burst of hot desire. He lifted his head, eyes meeting hers. "Emma," he breathed.

Her stomach fluttered with a thousand butterflies. God help her, she wanted his mouth on her in the worst way. She leaned in, and that was all the encouragement he needed. His mouth crashed onto hers and she clutched at his shirt, letting the sensations race through her body to settle in a throbbing ball of need at her clit. With a little moan, she opened to the sweep of his tongue. The feel of his tongue sliding against hers acted like a spark on a powder keg. Flames of desire licked through her, burning her to ash. The noise he made in his throat as he pulled her flush added fuel to the fire. No man had ever kissed her like this. With ferocity. With possessiveness. *Like she mattered.* As long as she lived, she'd never forget this sensation.

Some far-off rational part of her brain yelled at her to stop this. Push him away. But how could she when it was so good? He lifted his head, eyes smoldering.

"What was that?" she murmured, not trusting herself to speak.

"Worth the wait," he mumbled back as he angled his head to hers again.

Her hands looped around his neck and he caressed the length of her back, bringing his hands to cup her ass and pull her against his erection. She ground into him with an animal fierceness that surprised her and he responded with a dizzying kiss, tongue swirling hers, taking her higher and higher. Sweet Jesus, she could drop and fuck him in the grass right here.

He moved to her neck, breath hot on her skin. "You're everything I imagined. You light me up. I've wanted to kiss you for ages."

His words washed over her. Her hand slid over his shoulders, down his side, and slipped inside his jeans.

"I want you right here, Emma," he rasped.

She trembled with need. Her body screamed yes. Instinctively, she knew that he could take her to heights she'd only dreamed of. That he'd ruin her for anyone else. And she couldn't risk that. The thought put ice through her heart. She had to exercise common sense, even though it meant lonely nights with nothing but her electric friend.

She stepped back, gulping for air. "We can't do this."

His eyes swirled with lust, then filled with confusion. Then hurt. "Why not?"

She pressed her hands to her flaming cheeks, trying to find the words. "You're a player for starters. For seconds I live in Kansas City, and for thirds, I'm here in a professional capacity."

"And fourths you're a big chicken." His voice was flat. Hard.

And it stung. The accusation hung in the air between them. She shut her eyes, drawing strength from her toes.

"How many times do I have to tell you I'm not that person anymore?" A muscle ticked above his jaw. "I know you feel what's between us, Emma."

His words twisted her heart. He seemed so earnest. But she wasn't born yesterday. And yes, she was a big chicken when it came to risking her heart. "What's the point, Sterling? We're too different. I'm not interested in casual. I've never *been* casual. If we... If we..." She gestured to the ground. "What happens when the chemistry burns out? When you get bored? Give me the *it's not you, it's me* speech? I've never dated anyone from Prairie. No one would date me when I was a teenager, and now I'm glad. I don't want to be a source of gossip."

He opened his mouth, then snapped it shut, shaking his head.

God, why did this hurt almost as much as seeing him kiss Nikki Pope? "I'll get back to you on the poker tournament." She turned, and before she lost her will, left him standing in the field.

CHAPTER 10

S TERLING PULLED INTO a parking spot behind the police station. He needed the comfort of one of Dottie's special breakfasts. Maybe that would get his mind off the merry-go-round of confusing thoughts concerning Emma. Ever since he'd kissed her he'd been wound tighter than a spool of bailing wire.

Their kiss had rocked him to his core. Had unleashed so much more than desire. And it scared the shit out of him. He should be thanking her for saving him from himself. He'd come so close to forgetting about Johnny. But instead, he was just pissed off. For the last two weeks, she'd ignored his texts. And the voicemail he'd left with an apology. And the next voicemail a week later, asking when they could get together and discuss the fundraiser.

The worst part? He wanted to kiss her again. Over and over until he drowned in the sensation of it. Her taste had lingered on his mouth long after she'd fled, and he'd memorized every nuance of it. Of her. Of the way her eyes had turned violet and hazy with desire. The way the sunshine ruffled her golden hair. The defeated bend of her shoulders as he'd watched her walk away.

When Johnny had fallen for Macey, it was like he'd been consumed by an illness. Was that what was happening to him? He remembered it so vividly. Johnny looked at him and Jason one night when they were Firsties and confessed that he'd tear down a mountain for Macey. Whatever she wanted, he would be her hero. He and Jason had exchanged glances then, both knowing Johnny was a lost cause. He wouldn't rest until he'd married Macey. But then he'd gone and broken her – the woman he'd tear down mountains for. And Sterling couldn't square that.

But he also couldn't square this deep need to connect with Emma, to prove himself to her, with his promise to stay away from love.

Fucked. Up.

Main Street was still closed for construction, but week by week, new buildings rose out of the rubble. He made his way down the pedestrian path through the construction zones along Main to Dottie and Jamey's food truck.

Sterling stepped into line at the food truck, studying the menu.

"Coffee?" Brodie tapped him on the shoulder, offering a cup. "Jamey corralled me to run refills." He shook his head, as if not believing he'd been pressed into service, but his voice was indulgent.

"Thanks." He accepted the steaming cup. "Can I ask you a question?"

Brodie shrugged. "Just don't ask me to tell you what's on the menu."

"Fair enough." He took a sip. "I've been trying to reach Emma, but she's not responding. Everything okay?"

Brodie narrowed his eyes. "Yeah. You in the doghouse?"

Sterling laughed and shrugged. "Maybe. I don't know. I've got questions about the fundraiser I need answered. I thought I would have heard from her by now."

"Hmph. She left last week saying she was heading home

to work on it. Too many distractions here." Brodie narrowed his eyes, studying him. "You a distraction for my sister?"

He'd sure as hell like to be, but wild horses wouldn't drag that admission from him. At least to Brodie. "Do me a favor and let her know I'm ready to move forward with my own plan if she's going to avoid me. We're short on time."

"Why not let her know yourself? This wouldn't be the first time someone's had to drive into town to pull her out of a project. Hang on." Brodie disappeared behind the food truck and returned with an address scribbled on a napkin. "You might soften her up with a Special Breakfast and a side of sweet potato hash browns. Good luck."

GOD, SHE LOOKED good, all soft and touchable in yoga pants and a fuzzy pink sweater that hugged her curves. His pulse quickened at the sight of her.

Emma eyed him suspiciously, one hand braced on the doorjamb, the other poised on the doorknob. "What are you doing here?"

He tipped back his Stetson. "Time to stop avoiding me, Goldilocks. I'm not leaving until we have a workable project. We both know we're running out of time. It's nearly March."

Two bright spots colored her cheeks. "I had a project deadline for another client."

"So you couldn't return my phone calls?" he asked quietly.

She studied her feet as the silence spun out between them.

Damn. Had he blown it with her? His stomach sank. "Wait. I know. Our kiss had a devastating effect on you and you're not sure you can resist me."

Her head snapped up as she laughed, a musical sound that

danced over his insides. "You never give up do you?"

He cocked an eyebrow and grinned. "Never. Are you going to invite me in? I brought Dottie's Special Breakfast and sweet potato hash browns." He held up a sack.

She eyed the sack of food he held hungrily. "Are you trying to bribe me?"

"Shamelessly."

She dragged her gaze from the bag back to him. Did she feel it too? The way the air crackled between them when they locked eyes? Her lips parted and the tip of her tongue slicked her lower lip. Sterling's heart began to pound. God help him, he wanted another taste of her. Johnny's death be damned. He was only human. "Emma," he rasped, leaning in. She stepped back, eyes wary, but filled with something more. Something that made his heart skip hopefully.

Standing aside, she motioned him in. "Let's get to work."

He paused at the end of the short hallway. No wonder she loved it here. Fifteen-foot ceilings and a wall of west facing windows made the space feel enormous. If it hadn't been featured in a magazine, it should be. He approached the sturdy farm table standing between the open kitchen and a leather sofa, and dropped the take-out. One brick wall had been painted a deep turquoise. Mementoes from her travels were scattered across the room. But what caught his eye was the studio workspace in the corner. Half shielded by a folding screen, the chaos of papers scattered across a drafting table and a large cork board filled with photos stood in sharp contrast to the restrained elegance of the rest of the room. A red velvet fainting couch in front of the window called to him. Teasing him with possibilities of kisses and entwined bodies.

She was a study in contrasts, for sure. Who else was privy to this secret side of her? He turned back to her. "So who's the real Emma? The highly organized, everything in its place, all for show set-up?" He gestured to the middle of the room. "Or the free spirit who lives in the corner?"

Her cheeks turned as pink as her sweater. "Maybe I'm both."

Sterling approached her workspace and spotted a second bulletin board cluttered with pictures and words, even scraps of paper clipped from magazines. It took a moment to digest what he was seeing, but then he eyed her. "You've been busy."

"Of course I've been busy. This project is the most important thing on my plate at the moment."

It shouldn't have surprised him, but it did. "Why is this project so important to you?"

"Why wouldn't it be? Prairie took a hit this spring when the tornado ripped through most of the businesses. I want to do what I can to help everyone get back on their feet." She paused, as if debating whether or not to say more.

"But the ranch won't bring *that* much more business to Prairie."

She bit her lip. "Right. But Travis is a good man, and he got cheated in the election. He should have won. He's helped my family before, and I want to help him. And with my skills, how could I *not* help him?"

Her earnestness impressed him. All those years of close proximity, of mutual friends and shared classes, and only in the last few weeks did he feel like he was finally getting to know the real Emma Sinclaire.

"How come you don't have a boyfriend?" he blurted.

Her eyes widened, then narrowed. "That's not usually a question you ask someone."

"I only meant... I... shit. That didn't come out right." He grinned sheepishly, his skin burning. "I think you're pretty amazing, and any man who gets to know you…"

Her eyes sparked bright blue against her pink face.

Damn. Jason and Johnny had always agreed he was as smooth as they came. But not with Emma. Never with Emma. She set him off his game. "I'm sorry. I didn't mean to embarrass you. It's just–"

"Let's talk about the project," she said brightly.

He could take a hint. "Show me what you've got."

She hurried to her drafting table. "Sit." She gestured to the red couch and opened her laptop, fingers flying over the keys.

Sterling sat, but not before he perused her backside. God bless the inventor of yoga pants. She whirled, laptop in hand, eyeing him critically. "Why are you really here, Sterling?"

Something in her expression pulled at him. Her question shouldn't scare the shit out of him. But at the moment, he'd rather face down an army of ISIS militants than answer her. His palms grew hot. She'd always seen through his bullshit. And when they were young, it had been easy to laugh it off, tease his way out of answering. But he couldn't do that now. Not with the way she was staring him down. And he didn't want to. Even though that scared him too. He stared back, opening his hands in supplication. "I had to see you again."

Her eyebrows shot skyward, her mouth making a perfect O of surprise. She snapped her mouth shut, eyes narrowed. But her mouth tilted up at the corner, as if she was secretly pleased with his answer.

"This is what I've been working on." She came to sit next to him, all business. But he'd heard the quaver in her voice. And she didn't have to sit so that her thigh brushed against his. But she did.

At first, he didn't hear her. Her scent overwhelmed his

senses, but as the words and pictures flashed across her screen, he dragged his attention away.

"I've secured about a hundred grand in verbal commitments so far, but that's just the low hanging fruit."

"Wait. What?"

She turned to him, mouth drawing tight in frustration. "Haven't you been paying attention?"

"Yes." He drew the word out, scrambling to remember anything from the previous slides.

She narrowed her eyes. "Did you hear anything I was saying? Focus, Sterling."

"I am." Just not on her presentation. He could tell her in great detail about the freckle at the base of her neck. Or the way her blonde hair curled at her temple. Her breathing grew shallow and the air between them snapped with electricity.

Her pupils dilated and for an achingly long moment, he thought she might kiss him. But she cleared her throat and turned back to her laptop.

Her voice shook as she took him through her plan. "The diner is re-opening on the one-year anniversary of the tornado. A celebrity 5k and community pancake breakfast celebrates Prairie's recovery, and draws attention to the ranch – also part of the recovery."

He had to admit, it was brilliant. Tying the ranch to Prairie, so that one was synonymous with the other. Admiration for her swept through him. Her brothers hadn't been exaggerating when they'd called her a rising star. She'd listened to his feedback about the event not being too fancy, but she'd managed to incorporate enough VIP perks that her big donors would feel special.

"Lunchtime would entail a community barbecue and a raffle at the park with different levels of buy-in so everyone could participate. And the crown jewel would be a nighttime concert at the property."

He scowled. "But where's the poker tournament?"

"I don't see that working for this."

"That's because it's my idea."

She shook her head. "Not at all. You made some good points, which I've incorporated. But my goal is to raise as much money as possible for the ranch."

"And you don't think I know how to do that," he said flatly.

She stiffened. "You're not always the smartest one in the room, Sterling. Doing this kind of thing is my life. Bringing attention to people, to companies and their causes. If we're going to work together, you have to trust me on this."

Why wouldn't she listen to him? He had good ideas. He *always* had good ideas. "But you haven't even heard what I've put together."

Her brows slashed together. "You're not supposed to be putting anything together."

"Well I have. You didn't return my calls, what was I supposed to think?"

"That I was working on it?" her voice rose as pink crept up her neck.

"Just hear me out."

She scowled at him. "You are *not* taking over this project."

"I don't want to take it over. I just want to have a say."

"You've had a say." She stood and returned her laptop to the drafting table. He immediately felt the loss of her.

He blew out a breath, consciously softening his voice. "Emma. Please?"

She turned to face him, perching on the tall chair in front of the table. "Fine. Give it to me."

"I have a military buddy, Jason Case – whose military career was prematurely shortened by an IED. He's indicated he would like to be one of the first people to come through the ranch."

Her eyes widened.

"Maybe you've heard of them? Case family winery?"

"Who hasn't?"

Even people in Prairie knew the name Case. They were one of Napa's biggest names in wines. "They've offered to help sponsor the event to the tune of $100,000, as well as providing all food and beverages."

"That's extremely generous of them, but I've already brought Jamey and Dottie on board."

He charged ahead. "They've also offered to donate an all-expense paid trip for a weekend at the winery as the grand prize for the poker tournament."

She made a noncommittal noise in her throat. He could see the wheels turning in her brain and fought a triumphant grin. He'd never get her on board if he lorded it over her. "And the family of my third-year roommate from West Point runs a dealership in Indiana. They've offered up a new mustang."

She bit her lip as she processed that last bit of intel, then raised her head. Admiration filled her eyes. "I have to say, I'm impressed."

A thrill ran through him. He liked it when she looked at him like that. Like he was a hero. But then doubt crossed her face. "I'm going to have to go back to the drawing board in order to incorporate this."

"You know what? We need food. Let's discuss this over food."

She narrowed her eyes suspiciously. "Don't you have to

get back to the ranch?"

He shook his head. "At the moment, this takes precedence. The ranch won't happen without significant capital." He moved to the table where their food sat. Without waiting for her, he took out the boxes. "I know it's cold, but it will still be good." He pulled out paper napkins and plastic forks, placing one across the table. "Let's table this for the time being. I want to hear about *that*." He cocked his head at an exotic looking end piece by the couch.

"That? That's a Vietnamese fishing basket I had turned into an end table."

"Tell me about that trip."

She cocked her head, a disbelieving yet hopeful smile quirking her mouth. "Really?"

He nodded, placing his chin on his hand. "I'm all ears."

She launched into an explanation, eyes shining and face flushed with excitement. How had her family overlooked this part of her? The adventurous free spirit? Like this, she was captivating.

Sterling lost all track of time, listening to story after story. One-upping her with a few of his own, only to have her regale him with another adventure that topped his.

"And then she said with a very thick accent, *but I cackle in two languages.*"

He laughed until his sides hurt. "Good one." He put down his fork and turned serious. "We don't have to be enemies, Em." He itched to reach across the table and slide a thumb down her jaw. "We can be on the same side."

Her gaze grew heavy, as if she was weighing the new him against the asshole he'd been. His stomach lurched and he held his breath. Her approval shouldn't matter so much. But if love wasn't in the cards for him, he could at least have her as a friend. And right now, he desperately wanted that. To be the recipient of her easy smile. Hear her laugh. Even if it meant he never kissed her again. Never again lost himself in her kiss.

Taking a deep breath, she nodded and reached a hand across the table. "Okay. Friends. Not enemies."

He grabbed her hand like a lifeline, trying desperately to ignore the awareness that zipped up his arm. Reluctantly, he released it. "Back to work?"

Hours later they were no closer to a fundraiser. Emma stretched and stifled a yawn. "Do you always stay up until 2am?"

Lately he had, thinking of her. He shrugged. "Lots to nail down. I get energized by a project."

"It's too late for you to drive to Prairie."

He stood. "I can grab a hotel room."

She shook her head. "Don't be silly. Sleep on the couch." Popping up from the table, she disappeared down the short hall, returning a moment later with blankets and a tooth-brush.

"You always provide this kind of hospitality to your guests?"

"Sure. Prairie's a long drive in the dark."

He took her offering, covering her hands with his. It would be so easy to pull her close. Allow himself one more kiss before swearing her off completely. But he didn't want to risk losing all the ground he'd gained with her today. Emma as a friend was so much better than Emma as an adversary. The sparks between them were still there, but it was different. More satisfying than simply setting her off. He settled for caressing her cheek. "Sweet dreams, Emma."

CHAPTER 11

T HERE HAD BEEN no sweet dreams. Only tossing and turning.

I had to see you....

Sweet dreams, Emma.

The nerve of him showing up, softening her with Dottie's Special Breakfast and a side of sweet potato hash browns. Challenging her ideas, then in the next breath expanding on them. Asking about her travels, and regaling her with stories of his own. Of course Sterling would have a great sense of adventure. How could he not? Sleep finally claimed her in the wee hours of the morning. But at six a.m., she woke to the smell of bacon and eggs.

She padded out, bleary-eyed. Only copious amounts of coffee would help her now. She stopped short of the kitchen counter as the sight before her registered. "What in the world?"

Sterling stood at the stove, a dishtowel slung over his shoulder. Two City Market Coffee House cups on the counter next to a bag from Bloom, her favorite bakery. He turned, an easy smile crinkling his eyes. "Morning, Sunshine."

"Who are you and what have you done with Sterling?"

His laugh, rich and low, rumbled through her. "The second-best breakfasts in Prairie are at my house. My parents love to cook together."

A jealous pang twisted through her. By the time she was old enough to take notice, her parents hardly spoke. The housekeeper had made breakfast, or she'd been left to fend for herself, cobbling together cold cereal or leftovers. How different would she be if her parents had loved each other? Displayed any kind of respect or affection?

"Color me stunned."

Sterling turned back to the stove. "Mom made sure I knew how to cook a week's worth of meals before she packed me off for Beast."

"Beast?" Emma took one of the cups of coffee, pleased to taste a latte with no sugar.

"Yeah. Cadet Basic Training. It was a beast."

She laughed with him, warming at their easy banter. "Thanks for the latte." She waved the cup.

He turned, flashing another grin. "They're both the same. Turns out I prefer my coffee without sugar, too."

"Let me guess. You were just pushing my buttons that day?"

A devilish twinkle sparked in his eye. "Could be that pushing your buttons is one of my favorite pastimes."

"Why doesn't that surprise me?"

Sterling placed two plates on the counter. "Eat up, buttercup. We have a fundraiser to finalize today."

Emma dug into the fried potatoes. "I shouldn't be admitting this to you, but I still haven't figured out how to blend our ideas and bring my prime donors along."

Sterling leaned against the countertop, plate in hand. "What's the hang-up?"

"The most successful fundraisers don't just highlight the charity, they offer a unique experience consistent with the charity's branding."

Sterling forked a potato. "So you want them to see the ranch."

"Among other things, yes. I want them to feel like they're part of what's taking place at the ranch. Like their presence there is making a difference."

"Okay, so what's wrong with giving them a tour of the ranch and calling it good?"

"That would be fine if you want to raise a few thousand dollars. But I'm shooting for half a million. I'm reaching out to donors whose names are on the most important buildings in Kansas City. There has to be something more in it for them than a tour of your ranch."

Sterling put down his plate. "Maybe you're going about it all wrong. Maybe you need to get out of your comfort zone."

He was right. She never did well crawling the walls when she was stuck on a project. "You up for a little adventure?"

His smile dazzled her. "With you? Absofuckinglutely."

"Give me five minutes."

She hurried back to her bedroom, grabbed her favorite pair of leggings and her lucky brainstorm sweater. In the bathroom, she threw her hair up into a messy bun and quickly brushed her teeth. This would have to do. Sterling didn't know what he was in for, but already her creative juices were pumping. A stroll around her neighborhood was the perfect solution.

"Leave your hat here," she admonished as she threw a plaid wrap around her shoulders. "Do me a favor? Under the sink are a pair of canvas bags, grab them?"

He saluted her with two fingers and disappeared into her kitchen, to return with two canvas bags looped over his arm.

"Come on."

The urge to grab his hand as they left the building was

powerful. How many times had she imagined sharing this part of herself with someone? Only in her mind it had always been with a boyfriend. Not with a childhood nemesis turned colleague. As she strolled down the street thoughts of Sterling filled her mind. He'd surprised her yesterday. He didn't fit into any of her nice neat categories. The way he alternately encouraged her and challenged her kept her on her toes. But it was the heat in his eyes that chased reason from her thinking. When he looked at her like that, she wanted to throw caution to the wind. Wrap her arms around him and let him kiss her silly.

She'd regret it if she did that. He'd break her heart like he'd always done. And yet, the temptation to see whether or not he was as different as he claimed pushed every one of her buttons.

They threaded their way through the crowded market stalls, stopping to inspect winter greens and the last of the cellared produce. Apples, onions, sweet potatoes.

At the end of a row, she pulled up short and turned to Sterling. He stopped close to her, so close she could see the white flecks in his irises. "What don't you see here?"

He looked around, then landed his gaze back on her. "Is that a trick question?"

She shook her head, excitement spinning up through her. "Lots of local produce, right?"

He nodded.

"Local cheese, local eggs."

He looked around again, as if seeing the vendors for the first time. "I still don't follow."

"Walk up and down the aisle again. Tell me what's missing."

She practically bounced on her toes.

A slow smile dimpled his cheek. "Are you sure this isn't an excuse to ogle me?"

"I don't need an excuse for that, soldier," she answered boldly.

He cocked an eyebrow. "So you think I'm good looking?"

She pushed his shoulder. "Go take another look."

He turned, inspecting each stall down the aisle. The man had a great ass. A great backside period. Even covered up with a shearling. And she liked how he took a moment to study each vendor. But his confused expression when he returned told her she'd stumped him.

"I saw honey, soap, bison, lamb, and pork. Asian greens and herbs. Garlic, dried soups, and pea shoots. What am I missing?"

She grinned at him, bouncing up and down. "Longhorns. Do you realize what a novelty it would be? There are vendors who come from farther away than Prairie, and they're selling directly to the public. You could have a whole display about the ranch. People would buy not just because the meat was local and high quality, they'd buy because of your story."

He pulled her into a hug, kissing the top of her head. "You're brilliant. I bet Travis will love it."

She burrowed into his embrace before she could stop it. It felt so right, sharing this with him, brainstorming together, being with someone who truly *got* her.

He stepped back. "But that doesn't fix your fundraising dilemma."

She sighed, regret stealing over her. "It doesn't. But it's a start. Let's keep going."

After an hour of poking around the stalls, venturing into City Market Cafe for another round of lattes, and more pastries from Bloom, she stopped in front of River Market

Antiques. "This is my secret sauce."

He looked incredulous. "A junk store?"

"Anything but. It's a treasure trove and I've dreamed up my most successful PR campaigns here."

"Then let's get to it." He grabbed her hand, lacing his fingers between hers, and pulled her inside.

She should pull away. They weren't some married couple going antiquing. But the powerful grip of his hand set her body tingling. He strode through the aisles with purpose, stopping to inspect interesting objects, or to tease her with a wacky idea. She had to admit, his eye for the absurd rivaled hers. He stopped in front of a shelf full of tiki mugs. "What do you think, Em? I think if we opened a tiki bar, we could give Dottie a run for her money."

She covered a laugh. "You are truly incorrigible."

He stroked his chin. "I don't know... could be that grizzled old cowboys and umbrella drinks is a winning combination."

"*Stop.*" Her sides hurt from laughing. "You're too much."

She wandered farther down the aisle and stopped in front of a bin filled with prints from a local artist. This one had screen printed sayings and flowers over vintage newsprint and magazines. "See?" she held one up. "This is brilliant. You want to create cutting-edge PR? Look at what the local artists are doing." She flipped through the bin and stopped on one that made her heart sing. "Look at this." She held up a block print with the old Winston Churchill saying *Never never never give up*.

"I love Churchill," they both exclaimed at once, then burst out laughing.

"He's always been an inspiration to me," she admitted. "He always knew what he was fighting for."

"And he was able to inspire a nation to follow him,"

She snapped a picture with her phone.

"What are you going to do with that?"

"Instagram."

He rolled his eyes. "Don't tell me. You've got twenty-five thousand followers on Instagram waiting to see pictures of your coffee."

She laughed. "More like thirty."

"Then why bother?"

"Thousand."

"You have thirty thousand followers on Instagram?" The surprise in his voice tickled her.

"Social media is an integral part of PR. I probably have more followers on Twitter. It's part of why Royal Fountain likes me. I've made their ad agency young and hip again."

He shook his head, looking chagrined. "Hashtag Selfie Nation."

"Don't knock it 'till you've tried it Army man."

He scowled. "Social media is a waste of time, and gives too much information to the enemy. The less they know about me, the better."

"Get used to it. A non-profit like Resolution Ranch is going to need all the social media attention it can get. It's how your story is going to spread."

"Not if it means we're paraded around like monkeys in a circus."

"It's not like that at all. It's sharing your story. Resolution Ranch has a compelling story. One that touches many people. How many of us have friends or family who've served? More importantly, how many of us have friends or family who've come home injured? Or died?"

She must have hit a nerve, because Sterling's face twisted,

and he turned away. Her heart sank. She hadn't meant to upset him. Heck, she was only trying to help. She laid a hand on his arm. "Sterling?"

He stiffened at her touch.

"I'm sorry. I didn't mean to upset you."

When he finally turned to look at her, his eyes were dull with pain. All the air squeezed out of her lungs. His was the face of grief. Raw, unchecked grief. "Whoever you lost," she murmured, not knowing what else to say. "I'm so very sorry."

His face pinched and he nodded. "Thanks."

"I'm going to go pay for this." She held up the Churchill quote. "Take as much time as you need." With a heavy heart, she made her way to the cash register, paid for her piece, and sat down on the bench outside the picture window to wait.

When at last he stepped out of the door, he held a paper bag.

"Find something good?" she asked brightly. His cloak of sadness seemed to have lifted, and he shot her a devastating smile.

"You could say that."

"Show me?"

He shook his head. "Nope."

"Aww come on… please?"

He shook his head again. "It's nothing. Just a little souvenir." He traced a finger down the bridge of her nose and tapped the tip, stealing her breath. "Time for lunch."

CHAPTER 12

H ER WARM FUZZY feelings dissipated by mid-afternoon. Sterling Walker was as stubborn as a mule who lived to make her life impossible. He perched on the edge of her antique farm table, arms bulging as he crossed them. Implacable. Immovable. "I don't see the problem."

"Of course you wouldn't," she snapped, giving into the frustration coursing through her. "We're dealing with different groups of people. Beer and poker aren't going to cut it. Not for a group of donors who are used to naming rights."

His mouth turned down. "But that's what guys like."

"Your guys. Not all guys. I guarantee you the Belger Family Foundation will find that beneath them."

He side-eyed her as she paced in front of him. "Don't you think they're going to hate sitting on hay bales at an outdoor concert?"

She shook her head, turning at the wall and pacing back his direction. "Haven't you ever been to the Symphony in the Flint Hills?"

He looked mystified.

"This is my point, Sterling. Your thinking and world view are too small."

His head snapped up, eyes flashing. "You think my world view is too small? Just because I don't have a set of experiences that mimics yours? Come off it, Em. When you've crawled through the mud in enemy territory, or handled a sniper rifle," his voice grew thick. "When your buddy has died in your arms while you've waited for help – *then* you can talk to me about my world view being too small."

Emma's stomach dropped to her toes. Heat raced up her spine and her cheeks flamed. "I-I'm sorry," she whispered. "I had no idea. I didn't mean to imply…"

Shame sucked the air from her lungs. Sterling's friend had died in his arms? How could he get through a day carrying that kind of a burden? She couldn't comprehend the weight of that. Sure, she'd lost both her parents, and at least where her mother had been concerned, the grief had been overwhelming. But having a friend die in her arms? Like Luci? Or one of her sisters-in-law? She'd be wrecked.

She snuck a glance at Sterling, awe filling her. Pain pulled his face taut, and his eyes were lost in a far-off memory. "Sterling?"

He pulled her into a tight embrace, tucking her under his chin. She squeezed back, just as hard. Time slowed. It could have been ten minutes or an hour that they stayed that way. All she knew was that she was grateful for the way Sterling's heart pounded steady and strong beneath her ear.

"I'm sorry. I never should have said that."

His hand went to her head, fingers digging into her hair, rubbing in concentric circles. "It's okay. I overreacted."

She shook her head. "No. It's not. My first response is to always get defensive around you."

"Emma, you don't have to–"

"No. I do. You always had to point out that you were better than me. Cleverer, smarter. More successful. Never interested in what I had to say. And I, and I… wanted so badly to show you otherwise. Sometimes I forget it's not like that anymore."

He tightened his embrace. "Hush. I was a prick at seventeen. Cocky and full of myself." He leaned back to tilt her chin up. Her insides turned upside down when she met his intense gaze. "And I may have had a crush on you," he said gruffly.

Her chest tightened. "But you, but you... I don't understand."

He tsked, shaking his head. "I thought we went over this a few weeks ago. My opinion hasn't changed. On both counts."

Her heart galloped as she stared into his gray eyes. It would be so easy to kiss him. She only had to stand on tiptoe. Heat flooded her, rushing through her body like a wildfire to settle in her clit which throbbed insistently. She let out a shaky breath. She would just have to ignore the tap dancing in her stomach, the tightening of her nipples, the longing to have him stroke her to the point she forgot her name.

He abruptly stepped back, running a hand through his close-cropped hair. "So, tell me about the symphony?"

She fought a wave of disappointment. "Every year the Kansas City Symphony plays a concert at different ranches in the Flint Hills. It's a huge event. But they also have way more than hay bales. There are VIP tickets for seating and dining, and families bring picnics. It's too late for this year, but I think any number of the ranches around Prairie would be excellent candidates. They typically have five to seven thousand attendees."

Sterling let out a low whistle.

"It's rustic, but dignified. More Jane Austin than Buffalo Bill."

"Okay, I could get behind that." He crossed his arms. "But I still want a poker tournament."

"Enough with the poker tournament, already. Is there anything else you and your buddies are passionate about?"

"Easy. Army-Navy game."

An idea popped into her head. "That's it." She clapped her hands. "That's what pulls the pieces together. We need to play up the Army-Navy rivalry. Travis and Cash are former SEALs, right?"

He nodded.

"You and Cassie are Army. What if we host an Army-Navy contest? Place your money on your favorite branch, and the winner can be announced at the concert. We can have two tiers of raffles, people who bet on the winning branch are eligible for the grand prize raffle. But there are still good prizes for the losing branch. Everybody wins."

"You're brilliant." Sterling caught her up and swung her around, narrowly missing the couch. "I love it!" he laughed. The sound slithered through her lighting her senses. Sterling let her down slowly but didn't let her go. Her heart beat erratically as she met his molten gaze. It sizzled her blood.

She licked her lips and dragged her eyes away. "We need to set up an Army-Navy game." Her voice didn't sound like her own. It was a breathless, huskier version of herself. "I have an old boyfriend who plays first base for the Kansas City Kings. I can contact him about an exhibition game. Early April is just before the regular season. They may be able to squeeze us in. It would be huge visibility for the ranch."

"No" He shook his head, mouth turning down. "No way." Sterling's voice was hard. Emphatic. And brooked no argument.

"Why not? We could fill the bleachers at the high school and then some. Raffle away that Mustang your friend promised."

He grunted noncommittally. "Why not get the football team?"

"I don't have connections on the football team."

"Find some," he growled.

"Why are you sticking your heels in the ground? This is a great idea."

"Not if you're running around with your ex, it's not," he bit out.

"What?" She laughed incredulously. "Are you serious?"

One look at the tight set of his jaw said he was. "Are you *jealous?*"

A muscle over his jaw ticked.

"*Ohmygod* you *are.*" It was so shocking it was funny. Sterling jealous of *her?* She shook with laughter. Laughed until her sides cramped and her face hurt from grinning.

"It's not that funny," he grumbled.

She wiped an eye, still laughing. "I promise you. You have *nothing* to be jealous of."

He captured her hand, pulling her close, and cupped her cheeks. "Yes, I do. You're brilliant. And funny, and beautiful. And I've thought about nothing else for the last two weeks than kissing you again."

She forgot to breathe.

Heat smoldered in his eyes, and when he spoke his voice came out in a rasp. "I know you've always felt the chemistry between us."

She couldn't deny it. Sterling made her want... things. Hot sweaty dirty-talking naked bodies tangled on the floor things. Her blood sizzled every time he touched her. "I'm just a challenge to you," she whispered, heart racing. "Another conquest."

"I would never play you Emma."

The conviction in his voice surprised her. Weakened her resolve as her heart kicked harder.

"Just give me tonight. One night between two adults who know and like each other."

Something in his voice cut through her defenses. She flicked a glance at him. Her mouth turned to sawdust and her pussy went slick with desire as she recognized the need in his eyes that mirrored her own. All she could hear was their rapid breathing and her pulse pounding in her ears.

"I…" Her voice died as he kissed her temple. Then her ear, nuzzling down her neck, setting off countless nerve endings. Making her dizzy with desire. "Is this a good idea?"

"We don't have to make this complicated. Just two friends enjoying each other."

"Everything about this is complicated."

He raised his head to study her. "Or tell me to leave and go home, and I'll never bring it up again."

Her heart stopped in her throat. If she sent him home, she'd always wonder what it would be like with him. She was tired of wondering, tired of walking around in a state of constant agitation. If Sterling was offering to scratch her itch… why say no? How many nights had she lain awake fantasizing about this very thing? She fisted his shirt and raised on tiptoe pulling him close. "I want you Sterling… stay."

CHAPTER 13

A FOUR-LETTER WORD had never sounded so beautiful, and he readily bent his head to hers when she tugged. How long had he waited? How many times had he dreamed? And here she was, in the flesh, pulling him into a kiss. "I swear I'll make it good for you," he murmured against her mouth. He could devour her, but he was going to savor every second. Every sigh, every caress. He'd waited too damned long.

But she had other things in mind. Her hands dropped to his belt buckle, and in no time, she tugged his belt through the loops, tossing it to the floor. She yanked his shirt out, sliding a hand across his skin, lighting a fire that wouldn't burn out until he'd buried himself balls deep inside her.

"I want you right here, Sterling."

The blood rushed to his cock, filling him with a primal desire to possess her, claim her. He captured her mouth, tongue licking into her sweet recesses with a fierceness that surprised him. She groaned into his mouth, and fumbled with the buttons on his shirt. "Yes. I want you inside me."

He slipped his hands underneath the waistband of her leggings to discover nothing but a tiny scrap of material skimming the valley between her luscious cheeks. "So beautiful," he muttered before taking her mouth again and squeezing her soft flesh.

She moaned into his mouth and pressed her hips against

the bulge in his pants, notching herself against his erection, moving against him. Her hands were everywhere under his shirt, squeezing and pressing. Christ, it was like he'd lit gunpowder. "Yes, just like that," she whispered as he tugged on her waistband and slipped fingers under the whisper of lace separating him from her pussy. She arched into him as he cupped her mound, a finger sliding along her slick seam. "Yes. Feel how wet you make me?"

Fuck.

Her words fired his blood. Who knew that sweet Emma Sinclaire had a dirty mouth? She tipped her head back, eyes glittering with lust. Something deep inside him unraveled. "Take off your sweater. I want to see your magnificent tits," he rumbled.

Giving him a slow smile, she complied, whipping her sweater over her head, then paused, hand behind her back. She arched a brow. "Tell me, what are you going to do once you see them?"

He gave her mound a squeeze, blood pounding at the way she arched into his hand. His cock was so hard it hurt. "First, I'm going to admire them. Then I'm going to lick them, and suck your nipples until you can't take it anymore."

Her eyes glazed.

"Then, I'm going to lay you down and taste every inch of you. And then, if you're a good girl–" He winked.

Her mouth dropped open and her tongue swept her lower lip.

"I'm going to put my cock in you and split you like a goddamned peach."

"Yes. Do it," she hissed out, bra falling away to expose pale full breasts.

They were gorgeous, but his attention fixed on the dusky

pink peaks, puckered into hard points, teasing him. Calling to him. "God, you're perfect," he groaned, lifting a hand to cup her fullness, skimming a thumb over the tight tip.

She shoved down her leggings wriggling her hips, and he paused to help her, snapping her lacy undergarment in two as he pulled. He wanted all of her laid bare before him. He walked her back until her legs bumped against the red velvet sofa. Gently he pushed her down, falling to his knees at her side, ready to feast. He raked his eyes over her form. She looked like one of those magnificent nudes in a painting, golden hair splayed behind her, curves pink and luscious waiting for the pleasure of his mouth.

He bent, taking a darkened nipple into his mouth, sliding his tongue over the tip, and again when she hissed out a breath, her hand coming to pinch the other one. He brushed her hand away, taking over, rolling the point and gently tugging. Her eyes fluttered shut. "Oh yes, just like that."

"Tell me how you like it." He wanted to explore every curve, every dip and crevice.

"I want your mouth on me," she whispered harshly between shallow breaths.

He tongued a path through the valley between her heavy full breasts, teasing the underside and tasting her skin in concentric circles until she whimpered, arching into him. "Sterling," she moaned.

He loved the way she said his name. Need and pleading wrapped in a husky sound that shivered down his spine tightening his balls. Her voice drove him wild. And her words. Her fucking mouth took him to the edge of his self-control. And still, he wanted more. "I'm going to need you to be more specific," he muttered into her skin, tongue sliding over her taut peak.

"Suck it," she uttered, a wild edge to her voice.

"Like this?" He sucked gently, scraping his teeth over the most sensitive part.

She arched off the couch, clutching his head to her. "Yes."

"And how about this?" He skimmed a hand over the curve at her hip and down to her slick pussy, sliding a finger through her desire to circle her swollen clit.

She sighed audibly, hips arching to meet his hand. Crying out as tongue and finger swirled simultaneously.

"That's it, baby," he said tightly. His cock ached with need for her. "Ride my hand. Let me pleasure you. You're so fucking beautiful like this." He sought her entrance, coating first one finger then another in her wet heat.

She writhed beneath him, raking her fingers across his scalp. He mapped her skin with his mouth down her ribs, sucking and tasting, loving the heady scent of her. Nipping the skin, then tonguing the mark. Across the soft swell of her belly to where a light thatch of golden curls covered her skin.

"Open your legs, baby. I want to see your beautiful pussy."

With a moan, she opened and he drew his hand down her thigh, pressing her wider. If he'd been a teenager, he might have come in his pants at the sight of her glistening pink pussy, swollen and waiting for his touch. His breath hitched as he lifted his gaze and met her eyes, dark and glazed with lust. "You are without a doubt, the most dazzlingly beautiful woman I have ever known."

"I bet you say that to all the girls," she whispered, a light flaring in her eyes.

"Never," he uttered hoarsely, giving into the sudden urge to bare himself. "Only you, Emma. There was only ever you."

Her eyes grew wide as she processed his admission. "I

don't believe you."

"I've never wanted anyone the way I wanted you, Em. Never." A crease formed between her eyebrows and she bit down on her lip. He stroked her thighs, bending over her. "You don't have to believe me. I'll show you." He pressed a kiss to the inside of her thigh, inhaling. Her scent intoxicated him. Set his blood on fire. He shifted, bending to taste her sweetness.

She arched her hips to meet his mouth as he tasted again. Her desire flowed over his tongue, balm for his soul. A homecoming. Diving deeper, he lapped her up, exploring every hidden recess, at last sealing his mouth over her clit, making love to the most sacred part of her. Her body went rigid and she cried out loudly. "Oh yes, that's so good. I fucking love that."

Her words spurred him on and he continued sliding his tongue through her wetness, dipping in deeper for a taste, then gliding around her clit, pouring all he had into her pleasure until she shattered against his mouth with a shriek and a peal of laughter.

"Oh Jesus," she gasped between heaving breaths, a goofy grin lighting her face.

"Jesus had nothing to do with that, darlin'."

She giggled and he kissed her belly, continuing to stroke her legs, her hips, the soft underside of her breasts.

"I hope you're not through," she uttered hesitantly. "That was... amazing."

"We're just getting started," he hummed as he kissed his way to her collarbone. Her skin was like satin under his fingertips. For the first time ever, he wanted skin on skin. Nothing between his cock and her slick little pussy. He wanted to slide through her wet folds, coat himself in her desire. "Condoms," he rasped. If he didn't ask now, he'd lose himself in the moment. He was already so close.

"No need," she murmured. "I'm on the–"

"Are you sure?" He didn't want her saying that just because he'd given her the orgasm of a lifetime.

She nodded. "I'm safe. You?"

"I've never–"

She grinned up at him. "Me either."

Fuck.

A first for them both. He gathered her up and dropped onto his back, dimly registering the scratch of the wool rug beneath him. "Then get your gorgeous ass right here."

With her hair tumbled over her shoulder, she pounced on his zipper, helping him shrug out of his jeans in one move. She gasped as his cock sprang free and then clasped at the root, running her hand along his length. For a moment, everything went mind-numbingly dim. "If you do much more of that," he gritted through a clenched jaw, "I can't promise you'll appreciate the outcome."

"Sterling," she said in hushed tones, as she ran a finger around the slick head of his cock. "You're… huge."

His chest shook and he gave her what he was sure was a cocky smile. "Like what you see?"

She looked at him dead-on and licked her lips. "I want to taste you."

He clasped her hips, dragging her slick center over his cock. "Christ almighty, you feel good," he panted.

"But Sterling…"

"Next time," he panted. "I won't last if you put your naughty mouth on me."

She huffed out a laugh and wriggled against him, making him groan. "You like my mouth?"

"Fuck, yes."

She rolled her hips against him, sending another bolt of lust straight through him. "Just so we're clear," she panted. "You like it when I talk dirty?"

"Yes," he groaned, arching his hips into her and pulling his cock through her slick pussy lips. "The dirtier the better. Use that amazing imagination."

She bent forward, letting the tips of her hair brush against his collarbone, as she pressed her hands into his shoulders, sliding her pussy over his cock and stopping when her entrance hovered at the tip. She gave him a dirty grin that went straight to his soul. "How 'bout this? I want to slow fuck you until you beg for mercy. I want your big cock to fill me up. And while I'm riding you, I want you to suck my tits."

He shut his eyes as they rolled into his head, clenching her hips hard to refrain from impaling her on his aching cock. "Now, Emma. You're killing me."

With a sexy low laugh, she slowly took him into her hot, slick channel.

"Oh fuck, you're so tight," he panted. "So hot." She clenched around him and drew herself up. "You're fucking incredible, Em."

So this is what mind-blowing felt like. As she set an achingly slow pace, he stroked up and down her back, spinning closer and closer to oblivion. This view of her, riding on top of him like some mythological queen, full breasts gently swaying as she rocked into him was the closest thing to heaven he'd ever experienced. He captured a rosy peak, sucking and lapping, and was rewarded with a sound of ecstasy coming from the back of her throat.

She met his gaze through hooded eyes and didn't look away. "You feel so damned good," she breathed, voice husky with desire.

He squeezed her ass, burying his fingers in her softness. "You, too. So good." He swiveled his hips, grinding against her, stroking her back, and filling his mouth with her tits as she took them nearer and nearer to the edge. Her pants turned to soft moans, pitching higher and higher as he thrust into her hot, tight pussy.

"Sweetheart," he warned. "I can't take much more of this."

She clenched her walls around his cock and rode him harder. "Then don't hold back." She bent and took his mouth, sweeping her tongue against his as she increased their pace. He groaned as he thrust with her giving everything he had. She cried out into his mouth, body trembling uncontrollably. The waves of her orgasm gripped his cock and sent him over the edge in an explosion of white light that ripped through him, balls to neck, blinding him as he came with a shout. And still they rocked together, riding the tidal wave of sensation until at last she collapsed on him with a sigh.

"Wow," she murmured into his chest.

He kissed her forehead, a low chuckle rumbling through him. "If I'd known it would be like this, I'd have beaten down the doors to your ranch. Brothers be damned."

CHAPTER 14

S TERLING PAUSED IN the entryway. He'd been dragging his feet returning to Prairie all afternoon, but he couldn't wait any longer. Travis expected him back this evening. And the work was piling up. He pulled Emma close, reveling again at the way her soft curves fit against him, then calculated how long it would take them to christen the entryway the way they'd done every other space in the condo over the last twenty-four hours. His cock sprung to life again at the thought of taking her against the wall. They hadn't tried wall sex yet.

"When will I see you again?" As soon as the words came out, he regretted them. Their tryst was supposed to be a one-off thing. A means to slake the chemistry between them, not the beginning of something. Macey's grief-stricken face flashed in his mind. "You know... so we can work on the fundraiser?" he recovered quickly.

She stiffened in his embrace. "We? I thought *I* was working on the fundraiser and you were just signing off."

He laughed easily, relieved she hadn't read more into his slip-up. "Of course. But you still need to run everything by me."

She narrowed her eyes. "Don't think that this," she flapped a hand between them, "gives you license to take over my project. Now that we've set the general direction, there's not much for you to do."

That wouldn't do. She needed his ideas, their banter, even if she didn't realize it yet. "There's plenty to do. You need my connections. And anything taking place on the ranch needs to go through me first."

Two spots of pink bloomed high on her cheeks. "Is that so?"

"Definitely." He dipped his head to steal a kiss, sucking gently on her lower lip.

She softened, returning the kiss, then sighed. "Sterling, don't think you can sweet-talk me into letting you call all the shots."

"Who said anything about sweet-talking you?" He swept a thumb down her jaw and cupped her face to kiss her again. He flicked his tongue languorously against hers, hands sliding down her back to stroke her ass. "I'd much rather dirty-talk you." His voice came out rough with the sound of his rising need.

She notched her core against his growing desire, hooking her hands around his neck. "Mmmm. It won't have any effect on me."

He spun, pinning her to the wall with his hips. "None?"

Her eyes lit as she pressed back into him. "Give it your best shot."

His cock stood at full attention now, ready for a last go-round. "And what do I win when I make you come in under five minutes?"

She held his gaze and slowly licked her lower lip, then arched a brow, angling her head so the smooth column of her neck was exposed. "A cookie?"

"Only a cookie?" He licked a trail from her collarbone to the sensitive spot below her ear. "You can do better than that."

He slipped a hand underneath her sweater, fingers grazing the soft skin just under her waistband. "Your breathing gives you away. You're already turned on."

She gasped as he slid his hand down the front of her pants.

He nipped at her earlobe, letting her perfume permeate his senses. "What am I going to find when I slip my fingers under your pretty little lace panties?"

Her head dropped back to the wall, and she shut her eyes, biting down on her lip. "Nothing," she squeezed out. He'd give her props for attempting to stay cool. Her efforts were valiant. Cute, even. But he had her. He could tell by the rise and fall of her chest.

"Nothing at all?" he murmured, fingers playing with the scrap of lace that separated him from his goal.

"Nope," she squeaked.

"Liar," he breathed. "We both know how wet you are. How ready."

She made a noise in the back of her throat that went straight to his cock. It was the little things like that which set his blood on fire. A glance, a sly smirk, a sigh. Fuck. Who was he kidding? Just being around her heightened his awareness. Set his nerve endings alight. Made him want to do every naughty thing with her that popped into his head. He slipped a finger through the slick wetness he knew he'd find, grazing her clit. Her mouth dropped open with a sigh.

"You'll have to do better at resisting than that, sweetheart."

"I am impervious to your charms." She took in a ragged breath and bit down on her lower lip again.

He laughed low. "Are you?" He slipped a finger inside her, grinning as she rolled her hips and sighed. "So I should stop now and go home?" He pulled out, sliding his desire slicked finger around her clit before removing his hand entirely.

Her eyes flew open as she gasped, then she narrowed her eyes, reaching for his belt buckle. "You still only win a cookie," she hissed breathlessly as she buried her hand in his pants and stroked his hard cock.

He laughed, then lowered his head to hers, claiming her mouth in a searing kiss that left both of them breathless. "You like the game as much as I do, sweetheart. Like going toe to toe with me. You love the challenge and the sparring. The difference is, I can admit it. Now put your leg around me and let me fuck you."

She gave a slow pull on his cock, squeezing his length. Fuck. Everything she did to him made him see stars. He shoved down his pants, then yanked on her leggings, pulling the damn things off with a ferocity that surprised him. He wanted her to see them here every time she walked in the door. Hitching an arm underneath her knee and bringing it to his hip, he pressed her into the wall. She wrapped her other leg around him and he clapped her hips, bringing her down on his length. They both cried out together.

"That's it, right there," she gasped, pressing her forehead against his.

"You like watching, don't you?" he grunted, pushing into her then pulling out slowly. "You like seeing my cock fill you up?"

She gripped him with vice-like strength. "Yes," she moaned, her tone of voice telling him she was close.

For a moment, his breath caught in his throat as he watched his cock disappear into her pussy. The way she moved on him sent waves of desire racing up the back of his legs. So many firsts with her. He brushed away the wave of emotion that bubbled up from a hidden part of himself and concentrated on pleasing her, on stroking her clit until she cried out from the joy of it.

He braced a hand against the wall by her head, and with the other, cupped her neck drawing her mouth to his, sweeping his tongue into her mouth and filling her. Her legs squeezed his hips and tightened around him as she kissed him back with equal fervor, moaning as they soared higher until she shattered on his cock with a cry. His belly tightened and the most intense orgasm exploded through him, spotting his vision and nearly buckling his knees. "Holy smokes, Emma. I've never, I've never–" he caught himself and let out a harsh sigh.

"Never what?" she murmured, running her hand through his hair.

He shoved the feelings back to the hole they'd crawled out of. He could never tell her that in a moment of sex-induced weakness he'd thought about forever. "I'm never gonna taste anything as good as that cookie." He winked and gave her sweet ass a little pinch as he helped her stand on her feet.

She gently socked him on the shoulder. "Ass. You better hope I don't put salt on it."

He bent to retrieve his pants. "Even salt can't diminish the taste of victory."

Her eyes turned soft. "I had a nice weekend, Sterling."

His throat squeezed painfully. Regret filled him as the words left his mouth. "You know we can't do this again."

She let out a little sigh and dropped her head, nodding stiffly. "I know."

There was so much meaning there. So many words left unspoken. His heart twisted hard in his chest, and a cold ache seeped in to replace the warm buzz of post-sex bliss. For a heart-stopping moment, he considered taking back his words. But then the picture of Macey and Sophie, bent and broken at Johnny's graveside, slammed into his mind with the force of a sledgehammer. This was the right thing, even if it sucked at the moment. A little time apart and it would be like nothing had happened between them anyway.

She gave him a small smile "You're bad for my work schedule."

Shit. He didn't like this. Didn't like the flash of pain he saw in her eyes before she hid it with a smile. Didn't want to go home to his cold trailer and his cold sheets. And that was very dangerous. "It's for the best." A woman like Emma could make him forget everything, and that would ruin them both. In spite of that, his tongue seemed to have a mind of its own. And his body seemed to be more interested in staying rooted to the spot, touching Emma. "I have Guard duty next weekend, and then Travis, Cash, Weston and I leave for a week to go observe the Horses Helping Heroes organization in Montana."

She raised an eyebrow, a ghost of a smile curving her mouth. "I guess you'll just have to wait a little longer to see what I have planned, then."

He appreciated her attempt to push his buttons. Put them on more even footing as they said their goodbyes. But the only buttons he wanted pushed had to do with burying his cock deep inside her one last time. And the fact that those buttons wouldn't be pushed ever again left him... sad. He drew a finger down her cheek, imprinting her softness into his memory. "I'll call you."

"No need to."

The look she shot him told him she didn't believe he'd

call even once. That stung. He wasn't an asshole. Screw that. He would call her every damned day just to show her he could be a gentleman about this. That they could still be friends. "What if I want to?"

She shrugged, mouth quirking like she was trying to cover a smile as she pushed him toward the door. "Goodbye, Sterling."

CHAPTER 15

EMMA'S PHONE BUZZED from its place on the console. It vibrated again as she pulled into the parking lot across the street from the construction zone surrounding Dottie's Diner. Putting on the brake, she glanced at the number.

Sterling.

Nervous energy zipped through her stomach. To her eternal surprise, he'd called every day this week, often leaving laugh-out-loud messages. And while she'd never admit it to him, she liked the way his voice made her insides vibrate with something close to anticipation. And she loved the way he touched her. She'd never been with anyone who made her feel so alive, so uncontrolled and wanton. Sterling knew a side of her no one else did. Had encouraged it. Seemed to feed off it.

But he'd also made it clear that their slide into sexy times was nothing more than an itch to be scratched. Sterling couldn't be serious for love or money. So she'd sat on her hands, turned off the ringer, left the phone across the room to avoid temptation. But now that she was back in Prairie, she couldn't in good conscience avoid him. He'd see her marketing plan in action when he returned the following week. She could at least give him a heads up. Her heart began to pound as she reached for the phone. "Yes?" she asked a little too breathlessly.

His rich laugh lit nerve endings all the way to her pussy.

"Couldn't hold out any longer, huh?"

"This is me rolling my eyes."

He laughed again. "I *knew* you missed me."

"Hmm." She couldn't keep the smile off her face. Words formed on the tip of her tongue. *Tell me about your week.* But that would take things between them into dangerous territory. "I was just getting ready to grab a cup of coffee at the food truck."

"Oh?"

"I'm meeting my photographer over at the ranch this morning."

"But I'm not there."

Was she imagining the pout in his voice? "But Travis and Cash and Kate are. It'll be fine. When you get back into town next week, I'll have a stack of publicity materials to show you."

"Oh." He definitely sounded disappointed.

"Everything okay?"

"Sure, sure." He paused. "If you run into any issues, you know where to find me."

"I didn't think people took phone calls on Guard duty?"

"Not usually. But you know. If it's an emergency…" his voice trailed off.

She bit her lip to keep from giggling. "Of course. Thanks."

"Great. Is there anything else you need?"

"You called *me*. Is there anything else *you* need?"

"No, no. Just making sure everything's okay."

What was going on with him? He sounded… nervous. "Sterling?"

"Yes?"

"Be safe this weekend."

"I knew you missed me." The cockiness was back in his voice.

"Goodbye, Sterling," she said, shaking her head as she crossed the street to the food truck.

Her sister-in-law, Jamey, waved her over to one of the picnic tables. "Em, you know Lydia and Emmaline, right?"

She nodded. They'd been within a few years of each other at the high school. She sat, taking the cup of coffee Jamey held out. "What's up?"

"We've been catching up," Jamey said. "Emmaline and Lydia are thinking of teaming up to create a line of western wear."

"Oh?" Emma perked up. She appreciated her big accounts, but nothing got her excited like helping new businesses. "How can I help?"

"Branding for starters." Lydia pushed a paper napkin toward her. "You know how gorgeous Emmaline's dresses are."

Emma nodded. "And your boots." Lydia had made beautiful one-of-a-kind boots for each of her brothers' brides. She'd do anything to help these talented women get off the ground.

Lydia blushed. "So we thought the obvious starting place would be to go into custom wedding attire, but we need help breaking into the Kansas City wedding market."

"I can absolutely help." All she'd need to do is show a few pictures to some of the socialites she knew and the women would be on their way. Her brain was spinning with ideas. They could do a photo shoot. Maybe even at Resolution Ranch. Or at Jamey and Brodie's hunting lodge. They'd been talking about trying to break into the same market. "I'm going to rearrange my schedule next week and work from Prairie.

Let me see what I can do." She'd have to juggle a few of her clients and rearrange some design meetings, but her bosses would understand. And it would be worth it to help. "Have you thought of a name yet?"

Emmaline's eyes grew big and she shook her head. "I only make clothing. Everything else is Lyd's thing."

Lydia took a big breath. "I always liked the sound of Grace Boots, but I'm not so sure if that works with the addition of apparel."

Emma nibbled on a pen while her brain raced. "I'll think on it. Maybe this needs to be a collaboration between two different brands."

Lydia took a big breath. "I should also tell you in the name of disclosure, that I made a deal with Colton Kincaid."

Emma's eyebrows flew skyward. "Colton? That's quite a coup. I think the man has more groupies in Vegas than Elvis."

Lydia blushed to her roots and exchanged a significant glance with Emmaline. "Yeah. We... ah... have an understanding. But it's very confidential."

This was juicy. Colton Kincaid had been trouble with a capital T when they'd been young. Kicked out of the house when he was seventeen, he'd scrabbled his way to the top of the Pro Rodeo circuit and was killing it. He was a huge celebrity beyond rodeo, modeling everything from jeans to watches. If Lydia had managed to secure his help, that was huge. Emma couldn't help but wonder what the story between them was. "Let's talk more next week. Jamey, would you be willing to make dinner? I'm certain there's a way I can help all three of you. I'm meeting my favorite print photographer over at Resolution Ranch shortly, so I'll talk to her too. She may have some ideas."

Jamey hopped up and gave Emma a hug. "I *knew* you'd

be able to help."

Emma stood and topped off her coffee. "Figure out what night works for the three of you and send me a text. I'll bring my laptop and pens." Her phone buzzed again as she made her way back to the car. "Alex, how are you?"

"Still miss your sweet face. How are you?"

Funny. Her ex's voice didn't do anything to her insides the way Sterling's did. "Not that much, you don't," she laughed. "And I'm great, thanks."

"Aww, you know you'll always be the one that got away."

"Don't let your girlfriend hear that. Were you able to check with management?"

"Yep. Unfortunately, the organization can't do anything in an official capacity. Not this time, at least, although we should start talking about next year now."

Emma let out a small sigh of frustration. It had been a long shot talking to Alex about getting the Kansas City Kings to come out on short notice. Now that they had back to back World Series wins, things had changed for the organization. "I understand. I appreciate you asking."

"But there's nothing in our individual contracts that prevents us from coming out on our own for a charity event."

"Yeah?"

"So I talked to a bunch of the guys, and we're all on board. We think it's a great idea. My cousin Paul lost an arm to an IED in Iraq last year. Marki's brother is overseas with the Marines right now, and Rock's sister is an Army special-ist."

"I could hug you right now, Alex. This is great news."

"I'll settle for lunch when I'm back from Spring Train-ing?"

Six months ago, she'd have jumped at the chance. But

now, the only face she wanted to see was Sterling's. Damn him for getting under her skin that way. "Only if you bring your manager so I can ask him about next year. I'd love for the team to develop a long-term relationship with the ranch."

"For you, anything."

"One more thing? Connect me with someone in your PR department so I can start working on materials, and then let me know who's Army and who's Navy. I'll set up the rest."

"You got it, sweetheart."

Don't let Sterling catch you calling me that. Emma gave herself a little shake. Sterling had no claim on her. And Alex was a friend. "'Kay. I've gotta run. Let's be in touch."

She drove to the ranch floating on air. There was nothing quite so exhilarating as seeing a plan come to fruition. Especially when it was helping people she loved. Rebekah, her photographer, was waiting when she pulled into the space in front of the ranch house. "Morning, Bekah," she trilled, unable to keep the excitement from her voice. "I'm going to turn you loose today. Travis has offered up a horse if you prefer."

Rebekah shook her head, tilting her chin at the bags sitting at her feet. "Not with all this equipment. I'll be fine hiking around. Travis's wife… Elaine?"

Emma nodded. "Yes, that's right."

"Elaine offered to take me around on foot today."

"Great. Be sure you grab pictures of Travis, Cash, and Kate, too. We'll want a variety of shots to choose from in the promotional materials."

"Elaine said something too, about a Weston coming this afternoon?"

"Weston Tucker. He's our new Police Chief. Served with Travis. Sure, grab pictures of him too. Just make sure he's not in his uniform."

"Got it."

"And when we're done here, I have an idea for a new project for you."

Elaine, Travis's wife, joined them, looking adorably pregnant in a soft blue sweater. "Are you ready?" she asked. "Travis and Cash are framing the foreman's residence today. Some of the guys from town are coming to help."

"Even better. Too bad it's not warm enough for them to take off their shirts." Rebekah answered with a wink.

"There will be plenty of eye-candy. But why don't we start by walking the fence line? Then after lunch we can ogle the men." Elaine turned to Emma. "Would you like to join us?"

She shook her head. "No, I've got other work to take care of, but thanks."

The women ambled away, and Emma made a beeline for the foreman's residence. She'd bet money that Sterling was irritated the men were working on his future home without him. The least she could do would be to send him a few snapshots of the progress. When she rounded the corner of the barn, she stopped short. Half the fire department was there. Her heart beat a little harder as she studied the framework.

"Wait, guys." She hurried closer, searching for Travis. "Where's the basement?"

Travis looked over, hammer poised ready to swing. "No basements. Too costly."

Sterling couldn't live there without a basement. No way. Not after last year's tornado. "You can't do that. Not after last year."

Travis put down his hammer and came over. "It's okay. We talked it through. Sterling is just across the yard from us.

He can shelter with us if he needs."

"But what about the tiny houses?"

"We've purchased a shelter. Same one as your brother put in by his tree houses on your ranch. It kept everyone safe in last year's storm." He put his hands on her shoulders. "Don't worry, Emma. We're not going to lose anyone to bad weather ever again."

She nodded, worry slowly fading. Why was she worrying about Sterling anyway? He was fully grown. And had been in far greater danger than a freak tornado. "Can't help it."

Travis's face shuttered. "I know. None of us will ever forget what happened. I'm going to get back to work. Want to help?" His eyes twinkled.

"No, thanks. But I'll snap a pic and send it to Sterling."

"Do that. He was pretty upset we were starting on his place first."

"I can only imagine."

Travis started back toward the building, then stopped, turning back. "Hey. I'm really glad you and Sterling have figured out how to work together. You make a great team."

Something tugged inside Emma. "Yeah, we do. Thanks." She stayed rooted to the ground, watching how the group worked together, hands and hammers flying, an idea for the perfect housewarming present forming in her head. She snapped a few pictures and sent off a quick text to Sterling. He wouldn't see them until much later, but hopefully, he'd appreciate the gesture when he was able to check his phone.

Tucking her phone into her coat pocket, she wandered along the fence line before turning back and heading for the barn. The barn had always been her haven. It was the first place she visited when she came home to her brothers' ranch. And now that she could take little Henry out to pet the horses' noses, it was even more special. She slipped inside the barn door and paused, letting her eyes adjust to the dim light. Closing her eyes and leaning against a post, she let the warm smell of hay and horse settle in her bones. She couldn't get this in the city. As much as she loved her loft, part of her deeply missed this aspect of country life. The smells, the quiet, the communion with earth and sky. If only she had enough clients to afford a little place of her own. She could see giving up city life someday far in the future.

The quiet sounds of guitar strings echoed through the barn. Her eyes flew open. The soundtrack in her head had either come to life, or someone in here was playing the guitar. She held her breath, straining to hear. Whoever it was had skill. She'd worked with enough musicians to know. Emma shut her eyes again, letting the music flow through her, but after a few minutes, curiosity won out as her mind began to race. Opening her eyes, she slowly made her way down the center aisle, following the sounds.

At the far end of the building, around the corner, sunlight streamed through a second story window, casting a dust mote filled beam on a stack of hay bales. There, perched on one of them, guitar in hand, sat Kate.

Her long brown hair caught in a low side ponytail that draped over her shoulder. And she played with her eyes shut, chin cocked, as if she were really listening to her fingers pluck the strings. The sounds coming from the guitar filled the enclosed space, ringing off the walls. Emma's heart swelled as her body vibrated with the music. No wonder Kate liked playing in here. But Emma's jaw hit the floor when Kate tilted her chin, opened her mouth, and the haunting melody of *Shenandoah* filled the barn.

Her voice was husky and sweet, with just a hint of a burr

that would drive listeners wild and have them begging for more. There was such longing in Kate's voice. Such sadness. Emma's eyes welled up as the last note faded into silence. She should disappear. Leave Kate to her music. But she couldn't. She had too many questions. And how could anyone leave the magic presence of that voice? Kate's voice begged for an audience.

The young woman fiddled with the tuning, and then started into the familiar strains of a song Emma knew by heart. *Dance with Me* by country music's darling, Kaycee Starr. Late last summer, Kaycee rocked the country world when she'd suddenly canceled all of her concerts mid-tour and literally disappeared. Kate's voice was perfect for the song, like she'd been born to sing it. Emma whipped out her phone and pressed record. Sterling would flip to learn his employee could sing like an angel. She had to share this with him.

But as the words of the chorus rang off the walls, Emma narrowed her eyes. There was something hauntingly familiar about Kate. The way she sat guitar in hand, knee thumping to the beat, eyes shut, inside the music. Emma's heart kicked against her ribs as she gasped, puzzle pieces falling into place. "*Ohmygod.* It's you. You're Kaycee Starr." What on earth was Kaycee Starr doing on Resolution Ranch?

CHAPTER 16

KATE'S EYES FLEW open and a look of sheer terror flashed across her face. "What?" Her eyes went from Emma's face to the phone, and back again. "What are you *doing*?" She screeched. Only it sounded more hoarse. As if her voice wasn't used to working.

Emma stuffed her phone into her pocket. "I'm right, aren't I? You're Kaycee Starr."

Kate stood. "Ohmygod, you have to erase that. Right now." She held out her hand. "Give me your phone," she said hoarsely.

"What are you talking about? You're amazing. I should have recorded that first piece."

Kate's eyes grew wide. "How long have you been here?"

"Long enough to know you don't need to be communicating with pen and paper." Emma crossed her arms. "What's going on?"

"Nothing. I was just taking a break."

Emma smelled a rat. While Kate hadn't admitted it, she was sure the woman was Kaycee. "Why are you here? You don't need this job." She narrowed her eyes. "Is this some kind of a publicity stunt? I'm not going to let you take advantage of my friends."

Kate's shoulders drooped. "I swear that's not it at all. I need this job."

"No, you don't. You have more money than everyone in town combined."

"You don't understand. Please." Kate held out her hand. "Can I please have the phone? I'll pay you."

Anger flashed through Emma. "You think everyone can be bought? I don't want your money. I want to know why you're here at the ranch taking advantage of my friends."

Kate held up her hands. "I know it looks bad, but I swear, I'm not.

"Start talking." She'd dealt with high maintenance clients before. Half the time they manufactured their own drama.

Kate gestured to the hay bales. "Can we sit?"

Emma shrugged. "Sure." She followed Kate, and settled herself on a bale, studying the young woman, who paused to pour hot tea from a thermos.

Kate lifted her eyes. "Before I tell you anything, I need to know you're not going to go to the press, or sell my story to the tabloids."

Holy crap. White fury poured over Emma like ice-water. "I know there are some slimebags in show biz, but this is Prairie. And if you believe that any one of us here would sell you out, then maybe you should sneak back to your castle in Tennessee–"

"Kentucky."

"I don't care where it is. I thought you were here to help the ranch."

Kate looked pained. "I am. But it's more complicated than that."

Emma crossed her arms. "Try me."

"I'll need you to sign a non-disclosure."

Emma's heart went to the young woman. How lonely. The woman was what, only twenty-four? And already so suspicious and jaded? She waved a hand. "I sign them all the time in my line of work." She reached into her bag and pulled out a folder and a pen. She rifled through it to find the right form and scrawled her signature. "Here. It's Royal Fountain Media's standard ND."

She waved it in front of Kate, who took the form, scanned it, then carefully folded it and put it in her pocket. Kate took a deep breath. "How much do you know about me?"

"I heard you canceled a tour and disappeared from the public eye."

The young woman looked at her sharply. "Anything else?"

She shook her head. "I'm sorry. I'm so busy I don't pay attention to much superstar drama."

"No one knows I'm here. My sister helped me leave my estate undetected. As far as the paparazzi are concerned, I've become a recluse at my estate."

"You mean you never leave?" She shouldn't sound so incredulous, but was fame worth all that hassle? Not for the first time, she was glad her life was more… anonymous.

"Rarely. And it's fine. My property is well protected. I make it work. Or I did…" her voice trailed off. She took a drink and continued. "I- I… lost my voice. Ruined it, some people say."

"That's why the paper and pen?"

She nodded. "I had vocal surgery in October. And… and," she sniffed, blinking hard, then shook her head. "It partially worked. But they basically told me I'd never be able to keep the schedule I had before… before."

Emma gasped, covering her mouth. The poor girl. What heartbreak.

"I went back just before I came here, to see if by some miracle things had healed." Her shoulders slumped. "But no change. The doctor told me I could continue to try to heal through complete vocal rest, but that it was likely permanent damage and that I should, I should, find a different career." The last part came out in a whisper.

Silence filled the barn. A million questions filled her head. But none of them felt appropriate to ask just then. "But you sounded beautiful," Emma said softly.

Kate laughed bitterly. "I can't even tell. Everything feels so foreign. Broken."

"Well if this is broken Kaycee Starr, I'll take it. And so will a ton of other people, I bet. Question is, what do *you* want to do?"

Kate brushed a hand over her eyes. "I don't know who I am without a guitar in my hands. That's part of why I came here. I grew up around horses. And I figured if I could just make it through a day caring for the animals without breaking down, that maybe that was a start."

"So you came here to start over?"

"More or less. I figured if it was a place for struggling veterans, that maybe it would be okay to struggle here too."

"Has it helped?"

"Being here?" She nodded. "Yeah. Everyone's been great. But they don't know who I am. I'm just Kate here." Kate narrowed her eyes. "And I want it to stay that way. I can go into town and there are no photographers, no reporters wanting the latest scoop."

An idea formed in Emma's mind. "I'm planning a concert here for the beginning of May. You should sing at it."

She shook her head vigorously. "Are you kidding? I can barely talk. My voice hurts just from singing two songs. I–"

"But what if I could guarantee your privacy and security, would you consider it? Maybe it would help you feel better…

singing a little?"

Kate's eyebrows creased. "I'm sorry." She shook her head, eyes full of regret. "My voice is ruined. I wouldn't last ten minutes onstage."

"I don't believe that. The world needs to hear your voice, Kate. People would be thrilled to hear you. I'm no musical expert, but you sounded amazing just now. And having your name to bring attention to the ranch could mean a huge difference for Travis and Elaine."

Kate grimaced, shaking her head. "You don't understand. The ranch would be overrun with paparazzi. Everyone wanting a piece of me. Not to mention the crazed fans." She shuddered. "Travis and Elaine have been so good to me, and I'm so grateful for my job here. But I'm sorry. I just can't."

Emma's stomach sank. There must be a way to get her to change her mind. "Please consider it? The concert is two months away, you might have a whole new voice by then."

A tear dripped down Kate's cheek and she shook her head. "I know you don't understand, but I have to accept that part of my life is over. Please? I need your assurance you won't give my secret away. I just want a quiet life away from the gossip and the media. Please let me have that?"

Disappointment ripped through Emma. "I won't tell. But I think you're making a mistake. You can't hide here forever. What are you going to do when the other veterans arrive? Or when the press comes? Someone else is bound to recognize you."

Kate crossed her arms, her chin jutting out. "I'll stay in my house."

A knot of frustration pulled on Emma's shoulders. Some people could never see the forest through the trees. "So you'll stay trapped here instead of your own home, but you'll take everyone else here hostage to do it? How is that fair to Travis and Elaine, or the veterans they're trying to help?"

Kate looked pained. "Then just give me a little more time? I'm not ready."

Emma sat next to her on the hay. "Kate, the livelihood of the ranch will depend on its visibility. And I don't mean to be insensitive, because I can see how devastated you are. But the veterans coming here have been through the wringer. They've put their bodies and souls on the line in service to their country. They're suffering. *Please* think about how your actions will impact them."

Kate's face twisted and she hung her head.

"In some ways, we're all wounded, Kate. Every single one of us. We've all experienced loss. Hardship. I know you've heard Travis talking about that we can let those moments *be* our story, or simply be *a part* of our story." Emotion swelled through her as she thought of her parents, her brothers. So many in town who'd endured tragedy over the years. "Ask anyone in town. We've *all* lost something. Or someone. Some of us have come through better than others, but no one goes through life unscathed. We get through it by helping each other." She sighed. Was any of this getting through to her? "Maybe you need to think of this differently. Maybe your voice, even 'broken'," she made air quotes, "could help someone."

Kate nodded, but kept her eyes averted.

Emma stood, brushing her hands on her jeans. You could lead a horse to water… "Think about joining the concert. You know where to find me if you change your mind."

CHAPTER 17

STERLING PACED IMPATIENTLY through the barn. He itched to text Emma, better yet, hear her sweet voice over the phone. He'd only spoken to her once in the last two weeks, and he'd made a complete fool of himself. But it had been worth it to hear the laugh she'd tried to hide. And she must have thought about him too, because she'd texted several picture updates of the foreman's residence.

It still burned him that Travis had insisted his place be built first. He hated the bulk of the work happened without him. He'd make it up on the other houses, though. Guard weekend couldn't be avoided. And the trip to Montana to learn from the Horses Helping Heroes program had been invaluable. They all felt much better equipped to help anyone that came to the ranch.

But now he was home with the backlog of chores complete, he couldn't wait to see Emma. He shouldn't feel this riled up about her. This on edge. Like seeing her slaked some kind of deep need. But the fact that it had been two weeks since he'd felt her satiny skin under his fingers, or seen her cheeks pink up at something he'd said, made his teeth grind.

Distance was what he wanted, right? Out of sight out of mind? That's the way it was supposed to work. Instead, it had been out of sight, constantly on the mind. When his brain wasn't occupied with horses and guard duty, he kept replaying the way Emma's face softened when she laughed. Or the way her eyes sparked when she stood her ground. And the way they glazed when he kissed her.

He groaned as his cock stirred to life for the umpteenth time that afternoon. Sterling had half a mind to drive over to the ranch and carry her off like a caveman. But no. Better to save their meetings for public from now on. He'd made it clear that their encounter had been a one-time thing. Not for the first time over the last two weeks, he regretted it. The thought of her dating someone else, marrying someone else, talking dirty in someone else's ear, stabbed through him with a force that nearly brought him to his knees. He had to find a way to work this crazy chemistry out of his system. It was fucking with his resolve.

Two hours and a cold shower later, he pulled into the Trading Post parking lot. In spite of his efforts, anticipation wound through him as he pushed open the door, scanning the room for Emma. But his smile quickly faded when he spotted the wall of fame. All the photos, including the favorite of him holding the State Championship trophy had been replaced by an enormous Army-Navy fundraising scorecard and a "Sponsor a Vet" poster.

He crossed his arms, scowling. "Hmmph." Navy had raised twice as much as Army.

Next on the wall was a giant Kansas City Kings promo shot with the words "Exhibition Game March 29th."

What the fuck?

Emma had obviously been hard at work, but where in the hell was the information about his poker tournament? And when had this game been planned? Adding insult to injury, Emma sat at the bar laughing with her sisters-in-law *wearing a Navy ball cap*. His face burned like he'd been slapped. How could she? Although what should he have expected? It wasn't like they were dating.

He stalked over. "I see you've been busy."

She raised an eyebrow as she took a pull from her bottle. She had absolutely no business looking that sexy. Especially while rooting for the other team. "I missed you too, Sterling." She winked.

Jamey turned to him also in a Navy cap, gushing. "What do you think? Isn't this exciting? The Kansas City Kings are coming to Prairie. I can hardly stand it."

"I take it you're a baseball fan?" That shouldn't irritate the shit out of him, but it did. Of *course* Emma's family would all be baseball fans.

"I couldn't give two hoots about baseball," added Hope. At least she had the sense to wear an Army cap. "But I *love* the Army-Navy competition. It's brilliant, and I bet the ranch raises a ton of money."

Right. He had to focus on the ranch. Not on his hurt feelings. Couldn't she have at least worn an Army cap? Jeez. "What happened to the poker tournament?" He clung to his ire like a lifeline.

Emma waved a hand. "Calm down, Superboy. You still have a poker game coming, but exhibition game fell into my lap and I wasn't about to turn it down. And here." She reached for a cap on the bar. "I've saved you an Army cap." She handed it to him with a smile.

"Why didn't you check with me?"

Emma sighed, tossing a look at her sisters. "Because it isn't taking place on the ranch. And like I said, it all happened pretty quickly. There was no need to bother you while you were away."

Jealousy surged through him, coloring his vision. "What'd

you do? Have dinner with your ex-boyfriend?"

The light in her eyes transformed from amusement to pissed-off. Good. Now they both could be mad. She glared at him. When she answered, her voice came out clipped. "He's currently in Arizona at spring training. But he was nice enough to return my call and talk to his teammates – many of whom have family serving. And Alex's cousin had an arm blown off in Iraq, so he was happy to help."

"Wait," Jamey interrupted, catching Emma's arm. "You dated *Alex Jordan?* Why didn't you say so?"

Emma laughed, her face turning the prettiest shade of pink. "It was a long time ago." She slid a look his direction, lips curving into a seductive smile. "And it turned out he wasn't my type."

Fuck.

How did she manage to turn him on and at the same time make him feel like an ass? "I'm sorry. I was out of line." He pulled a smile even though he didn't feel like smiling at all. "It's great news and Travis will be thrilled."

Emma spun on the bar stool, giving him her full attention, and his chest warmed under her gaze. "This will be the kickoff to a series of fundraisers, including your precious poker game. Culminating with a day at the ranch and a welcome concert. How fast can you finish building those tiny houses?"

"That depends on how many hands we can utilize, and when the funds start coming in."

"If you can recruit the hands, I can coordinate the first deposit next week."

His irritation fizzled. "Serious?"

She nodded. "Yep. Take a closer look at the scoreboard. That's money already received. And not just from people in town. We're developing quite a following online and on social media. People want to see Resolution Ranch succeed."

"That's incredible. You're incredible," he amended.

She shot him a pleased smile, blushing to her roots. Damn, she looked pretty. If they'd been alone, he'd have kissed her.

"This project is important to me. And look, everyone's excited." She pointed to the pool tables where a group of firefighters stood sporting Army caps. At the same table, Weston and a few of the other cops wore Navy caps.

Sterling leaned into Emma, allowing himself a tiny whiff of her perfume. "Looks like you've started a feud."

"All for a good cause." Her voice grew breathless. "And it's good to give the town something to think about besides the struggle of rebuilding after the tornado."

"Then maybe we should show them what friendly competition looks like. Dance with me?"

She inhaled sharply, suddenly looking unsure and glancing over at her sisters.

Her hesitation irked him. Hadn't she missed him? "What are you afraid of, Goldilocks?"

"Go on, sweetie. We're just two old married ladies now." Jamey winked at him. "You two don't need to keep us company."

"You know you want to," teased Hope.

Emma's mouth quirked and she raised her eyes to the ceiling. "Fine," her mouth tilted up as she slid her hand into his. "All for a good cause."

Sterling's heart kicked up a notch as his little victory, and he led her to the dance floor, spinning her into his arms. She felt so perfect here, legs moving against his, hips swaying. He tucked her close, dipping his head to speak into her ear. Her scent went straight to his cock. She smelled like spring. And flowers. And sunshine and lazy afternoons spent fucking. "Miss me?"

She leaned back, eyeing him with exasperation, but still smiling. "Did you miss me?"

"Enough that I want to kiss you more than anything," he said, voice dropping.

She let out a small laugh. "Not here."

He splayed his hand across her back, spinning them and giving her a little dip. "So a weekend tryst in Kansas City is okay as long as there's no PDA in Prairie?" He pulled her up, bringing her face so close her breath warmed his cheeks. It would be so easy to kiss her now. Stake his claim.

Her eyes grew dark. She wanted him, too. He knew it. He recognized that lick of desire in her eyes. His balls tightened at the thought of taking her again.

She sighed. "Weren't you the one who said only one night?"

She was right. But after missing her for two weeks straight, he didn't like how it felt. His resolve pricked at him. What if he ended up like Johnny? Breaking her? He was just now getting his shit together. He couldn't risk it. And yet... his cock had other ideas. "I've been thinking about that."

"And?"

His heart started pounding, words bubbling up from his belly. "Come home with me, Emma."

"This is crazy," she murmured. "There are a thousand reasons why we shouldn't do this."

"And only one why we should," he agreed. "But isn't that one enough?" He looked straight into her eyes, half-afraid of what he might see. But her answer was there, shining out of her eyes, plain as day. Something deep inside him unraveled and his throat grew prickly. "Let's get out of here," he said with a thick burr.

CHAPTER 18

S TERLING PERCHED ON the corner of his brand-new office desk and stared out the window to the pasture. "C'mon Jason. I've seen you swing a bat. Just come out for the weekend."

"I don't want to be put on display. I'm on display enough at the winery."

"But you love baseball. And you'll be playing with guys who won the Series."

The phone went silent. He could just see Jason drumming his fingers against his thigh. When Jason finally spoke, his voice was tight. "What if I fall?"

Sterling shut his eyes. Jason hated talking about his injury. Except for those early days when he'd visited Jason at Walter Reed, his friend had never let on how he felt about losing his leg. That Jason was expressing worry now, spoke volumes.

Sterling's voice grew thick. "I'll be there to help you up. And so will your team. You're a goddamned hero, Jase. You lost your leg in service to your country. No shame in that. No shame in falling. The shame is in not getting back up."

The line went quiet again. After what felt like a full minute, Jason sighed heavily. "Yeah. You're right. Besides, I'm too pretty to fall," he joked bitterly.

"That's the spirit. You know I wouldn't ask you if I didn't really need you."

Jason's voice was light again. "I recognize that tone of voice. There's a woman involved."

Sterling roughed a hand over his head. "I swear–"

Jason cut him off. "A cadet shall not lie, cheat, or steal. Don't start now, homeslice."

Leave it to Jason to ferret out the truth in record time. "Okay, there is a woman." Jason's laughter rang through the speaker. "But it's not like you think."

"It's always like I think. All I can say is she must be pretty amazing if you're calling in favors for her after Johnny died. What happened to love is weak?"

"Nobody said anything about love. This is an old friend."

"Ummmhmmm... And let me guess... One that you've been 'friendly' with?" Jason's laugh filled his ear again.

"It's not like that."

"No? I don't buy that for a second."

"Okay, yes. We've been 'friendly'. But it's not like that."

Jason chuckled. "Sounds like you're in trouble, my friend."

Sterling pinched the bridge of his nose. Maybe he was. "It's more fun than anything. Easy. But I'm not in love."

"What about her? Don't be an asshole, man."

"I'm not, I'm not. We're on the same page." At least he thought they were.

"This I've gotta see. Count me in, then. And I'll talk to my buddy, Trace McBride. I'm sure he'd come help out."

"*Trace McBride*? Since when did you start rubbing elbows with him?"

"Since he stayed with a girlfriend at the winery about a year ago. He's a good dude. And ever since he made that movie about Afghanistan, he's been a crusader for veterans in Hollywood."

"That's fantastic. Emma will be thrilled."

"Emma? Wait. Is this the same Emma you went on a bender over in college?"

Motherfucker. He'd completely forgotten that he'd spilled the beans about Emma to Jason one drunken night when they'd been Firsties. Right after Johnny had informed them he was marrying Macey. He'd endured ribbing for weeks.

"Uh, yeah. We connected right after I moved back."

"Dude. You're so fucked," Jason crowed. "Wait until I tell Macey."

"We don't need to be adding to her pain right now," he said sharply.

"Did you ever think it might cheer her up?"

"How could it? It's only going to remind her of what she lost. And that we're moving on without Johnny."

"Listen to yourself, Sterling. We don't honor Johnny by staying stuck. And you know damn well Macey doesn't want that for us. We have to find the happiness he couldn't. How can we be good uncles to Sophie if we're living in hell too? That little girl needs us to be the dad she lost. We can't do that if we're unhappy."

Jason had a point.

But what if he spun out of control like Johnny? He couldn't drag Emma into that maelstrom. Wouldn't. A lump pressed against his chest. He wouldn't be responsible for destroying her that way.

"I'll take that into consideration." Code for shut the fuck up.

Jason's voice grew edgy. "How 'bout you do that? And in return I'll *consider* making a fool of myself at your Army-Navy tournament."

"Deal. See you in two weeks?"

"I haven't said yes yet."

"But you will. And I'll look forward to meeting Trace."

"You always were a cocky sonofagun."

"Damn straight." He grinned, feeling his old confidence surge back. He had this. He and Emma could continue on as friends with benefits and they'd both be better off for it.

Not two minutes after he'd clicked off with Jason, a photo text from Emma lit up his phone. The picture showed the Army line closing in on the Navy's and an underline beneath the total. His eyes shot skyward. Damn, she was good. 100k and two weeks left until the game. He fired off a quick text.

S: Wow! That's amazing. You in town?

A few minutes later his phone pinged.

E: Just a quick trip in for a few hours. I have to be back in KC tonight.

She hadn't mentioned coming back to town mid-week. He stared at his phone. "For what?" Frustration laced his voice, as a flash of jealousy streaked through him. Neither of them had spoken about being exclusive, but there couldn't be another man in her life. Could there? He shook off the feeling. His need to bed Emma was fucking with his head. They were having unprotected sex. That *meant* something. At least to him. But still… doubt ate at him. Only one way to knock that shit down. He fired off a quick reply.

S: Have time for an update?

Would she get that was code for something more than just a quick report on how things were going? Almost immediately, his phone pinged again.

E: Sure. In about an hour? I can't stay long...

S: No prob. See you soon.

The first thing he'd do after removing her clothing would be to tell Emma about Trace McBride. She'd be blown away. Trace would make their tournament much more high profile. Hope bloomed in his chest. Maybe with Trace on board, they could surpass their fundraising goals. Help even more veterans. A memory of Johnny slammed into him with staggering force. Eyes sparkling. Head tossed back. A wide grin.

Sterling's chest burned as his breath got stuck somewhere in his throat. He couldn't hear Johnny's laugh in his head anymore. He bent over the desk, splaying his hands across the surface, squeezing shut his eyes. Maybe if he concentrated, he could hear it one more time. The three of them tossing back a shot and laughing at a joke. But the silence in his head grew deafening. No laughter. No Johnny. Only the heavy pressing silence of grief. He sucked in a harsh breath and stood, hands on his hips, staring at the ceiling and blinking hard. "I'm sorry, man," he rasped. "I'm sorry." The door of his office blasted open, and he spun, heart slamming in his chest, hands raised, ready to fight.

"Shit. I'm sorry." Brodie Sinclaire towered in the doorway, hands out in supplication. "I didn't mean to startle you."

It took Sterling a minute to find his voice. He coughed and dropped his hands, heartbeat slowly returning to normal. "It's okay, it's okay. I should put a sign on the door to knock first. Can I help you?"

"Yeah." Brodie reached into his back pocket and pulled out an envelope. "Here."

Sterling crossed around the desk and took the envelope.

"What's this?"

"Just a little something to help out."

He opened the envelope, shock rippling through him as he studied the numbers in front of him. "I don't know what to say." Twenty-five hundred dollars from Emma's brother, with a note in the memo stating Army.

Brodie looked over his shoulder, as if to make sure no one was watching. "My little sister would kill me if she found out, because she expects us all to support Travis and the Navy. So this donation has to be anonymous." He grinned. "But I like you. And I've never seen Emma this fired up about a project, or a person." Brodie speared him with a sharp look.

"Thank you. This will be a big help." He extended his hand.

Brodie took it, giving an extra firm squeeze. Was Emma's brother trying to intimidate him?

"Let's consider this a gentleman's agreement. You have my support." He grinned again, a wild look entering his eye. "And if you hurt my sister in any way, I'll be waiting for you in the tall grass."

CHAPTER 19

E MMA PULLED INTO the circle in front of the new foreman's house. So was this what a booty call felt like? Or was this more? Her college roommates had joked about booty calls, but back then she'd been more concerned with her studies than boys. Did you bring a housewarming gift to a booty call? She glanced over at the neatly wrapped package on the front seat, then nibbled on a fingernail, nervous energy winding through her. She had no need to be nervous, it was Sterling. But she shouldn't be here. She should be back in Kansas City working on her other projects.

Driving over to Prairie in the middle of a Wednesday afternoon was completely out of character for her. And yet here she was, anticipation spooling tight in her belly at the thought of running her hands over Sterling's body. Of saying a thousand dirty things that in any other circumstance would make her blush to her bones. Of chasing after a release so powerful she couldn't think.

But it was *just* a booty call. Right? They couldn't keep their hands off each other when they were together, and sure, they'd had several late-night conversations, but they'd never been *intimate*. Shared secrets. Bared their souls.

Emma drummed her fingers on the steering wheel. Sterling was the closest she'd come to baring her soul, but he wasn't her boyfriend. He didn't want a relationship. And she couldn't do this commuting thing back and forth to Prairie forever. So it would end. It had to. A part of her chest hollowed at the thought. She *liked* being around him. Loved the way he made her feel like he only had eyes for her. But that was infatuation. Chemistry. You couldn't build a life on that. She'd witnessed first-hand the disastrous consequences of orbiting a person who made you feel like you were the only one in the room. At least while he was looking your direction.

Sterling had given her no reasons to think he was even remotely the kind of sweet-talking philanderer her father had been. Yes, Sterling was devastatingly charming. But they were friends, too. Her parents had either thrown things at each other or passionately made up. And when her father went on a bender, her mother would take herself to bed and brood. Not come out for days. And after he'd died, it was like her mother had died too – couldn't manage living without the toxic charisma of Jake Sinclaire to give her life direction.

Emma shook herself, pushing the maudlin thoughts away. None of her brothers had repeated history, and she wouldn't either. And attempting to put a label on what was between her and Sterling would only complicate things. And they'd agreed to uncomplicated. She couldn't help smiling as she grabbed the little gift to her right. Exiting the car, she skipped up the steps and knocked on the door.

No one answered. Where was he? He'd invited *her* over. She knocked again, more loudly. After a minute she tried the door. "Sterling?" She stuck her head in and scanned the office. The far door to the rest of the house stood open. Slipping inside and pulling the door shut behind her, she cautiously crossed the floor. "Sterling?" She stepped into the living space as he stepped out of the bathroom, freshly showered and in nothing but a towel slung low across his hips.

Her mouth turned to sawdust, and words vanished as she stared. Heavens, he was *fine*. From the top of his damp head, down his chiseled chest still glistening, to the tips of his bare toes. And he was freshly shaved. Her knees went weak at the thought of that smooth skin rubbing up against all her sensitive spots. And she couldn't wait to get her hands on that towel. She licked her lips at what she knew she'd discover underneath.

He pinned her with a hungry gaze as a slow self-satisfied smile spread across his face. "Couldn't get enough of me, could you?"

"Cocky much?" Let him think he had this under control. She'd turn the tables on him in a hot second.

"Why else would you come to town midweek?"

"Wanted to check on a few details," she bluffed. It was partially true, but if she'd really wanted, she could have asked one of her brothers to help her out.

"Don't ever play poker, Goldilocks." His stayed locked on her.

"You knew I was coming over, how do you know it wasn't purely for business?" she countered.

He cocked an eyebrow. "When has it ever been purely business between us?" His gaze grew heated as he raked his gaze down her body. She'd come straight from work and was overdressed for Prairie, wearing a navy pencil skirt and red stilettos. "You look amazing," he said, his voice taking on a husky note.

Her nipples tightened to hard peaks under his gaze, and the way his eyes lit, it was obvious to him too. "Thank you." The air charged between them.

"What's in your hand?"

"Nothing. Something I thought you'd like." She dragged

her gaze away, searching for a place to put it down. She crossed the room and bent to lay the simply wrapped package on the end table. Sterling's sharp intake of breath told her he'd glimpsed the lacy tops of her thigh-highs when she'd bent. She glanced over her shoulder with a seductive smile, not missing the growing bulge under his towel. "Like what you see?"

"You know I do," he rasped.

A rush of warmth pooled in her center as his gaze turned feral. She loved this. The chase, the back and forth, the drawing out the tension until they both couldn't stand it. She swallowed, relishing the waves of desire rushing to her fingertips, to her toes, making every part of her body hypersensitive, eagerly awaiting his touch. She brought her hand to the top button of her shirt, easily releasing it. "Would you like to touch me here?" She released the next button, and the next, drawing a finger down the exposed vee of skin.

"Yes." His voice was dry. Hoarse.

She freed the last buttons, and with a shrug, the silk whispered to the floor. The sound of Sterling's ragged breathing and her racing heart filled the room.

"You're playing with fire, Goldilocks."

"Burn me." Her skirt pooled at her feet and she stepped out keeping her gaze riveted on him, closing the distance between them in two sultry steps.

He let out a harsh breath. "Keep the heels."

The way he looked at her made her blood boil. She'd never felt so hot, so on fire. Sterling stood before her, body tight, clutching his towel like a lifeline. As if he'd devour her once he let go. It was heady, wielding this kind of power.

"I wanna bend you over the couch and fuck your brains out," he said, voice tight with need.

She let out a little laugh as she drew a finger down the

center of his torso, hooking it under the edge of his towel. "You'll get your turn, Soldier. But we have some unfinished business." He cocked his head, and she arched a brow, unable to stop a smile from spreading across her face. "Oh yes. I've been waiting very patiently." She gave a little tug on the towel. Not enough to pull it off, but enough that he relinquished his hold on it. "Time's up." She snapped the towel off, and his cock sprang free, heavy and hard and thick.

Lust charged through her. His cock was incredible. And her body flooded with endorphins at the thought of him filling her in so many naughty satisfying ways. She stepped forward, and his hands rose to cup her hips. But she shook her head. "No touching. Not yet."

"Emma," he half pleaded, half groaned.

Using her fingers, she traced a path from his navel down across the tight flat of his abdomen, to the base of his cock bobbing in front of her. Sliding along the sensitive ridge, she explored his length, delighting in the silky feel of him. An instrument of pleasure that she craved. There weren't enough days on earth to come close to slaking her thirst for him. She smeared the drop of pre-come over the engorged head, salivating at the slick feel. She licked her lips and glanced at him through her lashes as she dropped to her knees.

His breath came out in a sharp hiss as she cupped his balls in her palm while she ran her tongue along the underside of his shaft. She sighed as his taste filled her, sharp and manly. The scent of his arousal burned a path straight to her clit. As she took him into her mouth, her hand encircled the base of his cock, stroking up to meet her mouth. His palm came to her head, fingers tangling in her hair, and he moaned as she used her tongue.

When she looked up at him, her insides melted in a blaze

of desire. His eyes were riveted on her, blazing and wild, mouth parted with shallow breaths. She kept her eyes trained on him, taking in the hard planes of his face, now etched with the most beautiful combination of ecstasy and agony. Something ripped open inside of her as she locked gazes with him. An awareness that whatever barriers stood between them were being burned to ash. She continued to suck and lick, half-dizzy from her own desire and the power of what was building between them.

His fingers tightened on her hair, pulling, as he involuntarily thrust his hips, gently pushing deeper into her mouth. Still looking at her, his voice came out razor sharp. "I want you so bad right now."

She answered by taking him as deep as she could, until his cock pressed against the back of her throat. The feel of him filling her like this set her body trembling with her own unquenched need. But she didn't want to stop. Not this time. She wanted him to think of this every time he walked into the living room. A primal need to mark this space as hers swept through her.

"I'm close," he gritted, pulling harder on her hair and sending sizzles of fire through her veins.

She groaned with the beauty of him, imprinting this moment into her memory. The sound must have sent him over the edge, because he dropped his head with a shout, went rigid as a burst of hot come hit her and she swallowed, taking all of him until he was spent. Still gasping for air, he relaxed his fingers and pulled out, dropping to his knees and handing her the towel. "Fucking hell, that was hot."

She grinned at him, body humming. "Like that, did you?"

His eyes glittered. "You're not leaving here until I've bent you over the couch."

A thrill ran through her. "That so?" she couldn't resist teasing. "And how are you going to achieve that?"

Quick as lightning, he captured her wrist, turning it up. The heat returned to his eyes as he gently kissed the delicate skin, tonguing the flesh. "I can feel your pulse hammering," he murmured, keeping her gaze. "You're wound tighter than bailing wire." He moved his mouth to her palm, not breaking eye contact.

Her head spun as need drove through her with the force of a tank. Every cell in Emma's body vibrated, longing for more of his touch. He was right. There was no way she was leaving until he'd filled her completely. Satisfied the need for him that seemed to grow with each passing day.

He ran a finger across her collarbone, sending tingles across her flesh, making her nipples ache in anticipation. She shut her eyes, taking it in.

"Look at me, Emma."

She opened her eyes, pulse rocketing. He gave her slow smile. "You're so beautiful when you're turned on." He drew the back of a finger down her sternum, and traced along the edge of her bra, slipping down to rub back and forth against her tight peak. She drew a ragged breath, clit throbbing.

"And you're even more beautiful when you come. Do you want to come, Em?"

"Yes," she uttered, forgetting to breathe.

"Take off your bra. Show me those pretty tits."

A rush of hot desire pooled between her legs. His words torched her. She reached behind herself and released the clasp, shimmying the straps off her arms.

Sterling's breath released sharply as his finger continued moving back and forth over the sensitized tip. "So beautiful," he murmured.

"Put your mouth on me," she begged, not caring that he was supposed to be calling the shots. She wanted relief from the agony building inside her.

"Where?"

"Suck my tits, Sterling," she said boldly as another hot rush of desire soaked her panties.

He lowered his head, breath skating across her skin like a tease. It wasn't enough. She bit back a needy moan when his tongue lightly flicked across first one hard bud then the other. He went back and forth until her breath came out in great gasps. "More, I need more."

"Mmm?"

"Stop teasing," she said, need sharpening her voice to a point.

"Never," he murmured with a ghost of a smile, before taking her nipple into his mouth and giving her what she wanted.

She arched into him, clasping his head as he dragged his teeth gentle across the end as she sucked. "Yes, that's it." Craving for him chased all other thoughts away except for the need to have him inside her. She cried out when he raised his head and pulled them both to their feet. She swayed and clutched his arm, punch drunk with desire.

"Take those pretty little panties off," he said roughly.

She hooked a thumb through the elastic and peeled off the lace. Then grinned at his sharp intake of breath.

"You've been busy,"

She arched a brow. "Like?"

"Oh hell, yes." He reached out a finger to trace her newly bare pussy.

On a whim, she'd picked up an issue of *Cosmo* the week before and took some of the advice she'd found inside. So far, she liked the results.

"You're so soft, so wet." He spoke almost reverently, like she was a treasure. He split her wet seam, exploring deeper, spreading her desire across her swollen folds until he brushed her clit with feather-light strokes. Bringing his finger to her mouth, he coated her lips with her essence before cupping the back of her head and lowering his mouth to hers. His tongue moved slowly over her lips, tasting her before teasing into her mouth to slide against her tongue.

She clutched his shoulder at the slow sensuality of it.

"I love the taste of you," he murmured before kissing her more roughly.

She responded like a woman possessed, arching into him, hands stroking his back, squeezing his ass, as she kissed him back fervently, letting instinct and need drive her actions. His erection pressed into her thigh and she shifted wanting it where it could bring sweet relief.

"Not yet," he murmured as he walked her backward toward the couch. "I want you to bend over that couch in your sexy heels and show me that gorgeous ass."

Turning, she braced herself on the arm and glanced back at him. He looked positively predatory, cock jutting out, heavy and hard. She wiggled her ass and gave him a slow smile. "You mean like this?" Need tightened in her belly at his answering look.

"Spread your legs farther apart."

She widened her stance and shook her ass again. "I'm ready. Come put your cock inside me." Her pussy throbbed expectantly, and she cried out at the first touch of his cock sliding along her swollen folds. She leaned back, chasing the sensation, and he pulled away briefly.

"Sterling…" she squeezed out through a tight throat. "I

swear to God, I'll–" He cut her off, thrusting all the way home. "*Yes,*" she gasped, adjusting to his rhythm.

He slung an arm across her belly, pulling her close, supporting her as she ground into him. With each thrust, he touched a place deep inside her.

"Incredible," he grunted.

"Yes," she gasped as his fingers found her clit and fluttered against it as light and soft as his thrusts were hard and deep. The sensation was too much for her brain to hold. She spiraled out of control in an explosion of heat and sparkling light. Sterling was right there with her, thrusting deeply with a cry and grinding into her as they rode the tidal wave that caught them both.

CHAPTER 20

STERLING PULLED A big blanket over them and settled her on his lap. She sighed and burrowed into him, relishing the feel of it against her skin. "Mmmm. Since when did you develop a taste for cashmere?"

His chest shook against her. "Housewarming gift from Ma. Guess she knows what the ladies like."

She socked him gently on the shoulder. "There better be only one lady," she said sternly, then instantly regretted blurting the words. This was supposed to be a no-strings-attached thing. And if she'd learned one thing from watching her mother's mistakes was that you can't ever hold a man down. The second you pin expectations to them would be the second they ran for the hills.

Sterling stiffened under her, and she shut her eyes, bracing for the gentle let-down. "There's no one else, Emma."

Steeling herself for what she'd see in his eyes, she lifted her head. "I didn't mean to, I'm sorry. I shouldn't have–"

Sterling placed a finger across her lips, shaking his head. "Shh. We've never talked about it, but for the record, there's no one else."

His words shouldn't delight her, but they did. Warmth spilled across her chest and she snuggled closer.

He sighed deeply and continued. "I would never, I'd never dream of…" He coughed, shaking his head again. When he spoke again, his voice was thick. "There's only you Emma. I can't give you much, but you have my word on that."

The air grew tense. Heavy. Uncomfortable. Like neither of them wanted to acknowledge what was hanging between them. She'd never ask for more than he could give, and if this was it… well, for now, that was okay. She leaned back and grabbed the package she'd placed on the end table. "Here." She handed him the gift. "Not as warm and fuzzy as this blanket, but I hope you'll like it."

Her heart squeezed anxiously as he slowly unwrapped the brown paper, then released in a rush of warmth as he breathed out, arms encircling her tightly. When he spoke, his voice was gravelly. "I love it."

"I was at River Market Antiques the other day, and there was another *Never Give Up* in the bins." Her face burned. "I couldn't resist."

"It's perfect. I'll hang it in the office." He pressed a kiss to her temple. "So. I have news for you."

"Yes?"

"Big news." He smirked.

All right. If he wanted to play coy, she'd go along with it. "How big?"

His smirk spread into a grin. "Huge."

She giggled. "Let me guess. Your fundraising ace in the hole?"

He lifted a shoulder. "I've told you a thousand times, Rangers lead the way."

"Except when they play Navy in football?" she teased, knowing that would get a rise out of him.

He pinched her playfully. "Even then. Never, never, never give up. Right?" He winked. "But since you asked, Army will crush Navy in fundraising."

She straightened, fully alert. "Those are big words. You got the goods?"

He rolled his hips beneath her. "You doubt me, Goldilocks?"

"Show me the money, cowboy."

"I have two words for you."

He looked like the cat that just ate the canary, but she couldn't resist egging him on just a bit more. "Let me guess… lottery ticket."

He leaned back, chuckling. "I guess you could call him that."

"Him?"

He waggled his eyebrows, clearly enjoying this way too much. "Trace McBride."

She squirmed off his lap and onto her knees. "*What?*"

"Did I remind you never to play poker?"

"You got *Trace McBride?*" she squealed. Trace McBride was only the hottest ticket in Hollywood right now, coming off three seasons of consecutive blockbusters. "For real?"

Sterling scowled at her. "You don't have to be *that* excited."

She bounced on the couch, blanket slipping off her shoulder. "Are you kidding? It's *Trace McBride.* Do you know what that's going to do for the visibility of Resolution Ranch?" Even as she spoke the words, warning bells sounded in her head. Kate was here to hide from the paparazzi. Trace McBride was as big a draw as Kaycee Starr, if not more. Paparazzi would be crawling through Prairie while Trace was here, and that would be bad for Kate. The realization dampened her enthusiasm.

"What was *that* look for?" Sterling asked, concern lacing his voice. "Did I just fuck up?"

She shook her head. "No. *No.* This is incredible. But I have news for you too."

He shifted, bracing an elbow on the back of the couch. "You've been talking to one of McBride's former girlfriends?"

"No, nothing like that, but it's big. As big as yours."

"Lay it on me." Curiosity lit his eyes.

She liked seeing him like this. Excited. The shadow of grief that regularly haunted his eyes, gone for the moment.

"Can you keep a secret?"

"Of course."

"I mean it. This is very confidential. I need to know I can trust you."

"My top-secret security clearance isn't enough?"

She hopped off the couch and grabbed her phone out of her bag. Settling herself back under the blanket, she pulled up the video she'd taken of Kate. "Look who it is. And listen."

He shot her a confused look. "I don't understand. It's obviously Kate."

"Just listen."

He hit play, and Kate's husky sweet voice played back at them. He paused the video to look at her, still confused.

"Keep listening. And imagine blonde hair."

He pressed play again, then after a minute, stiffened. "Holy shit. She's Kaycee Starr, isn't she?" He glanced at her for confirmation.

"Yes. And I'm trying to convince her to give a concert here."

He put down the phone. "Does Travis know?"

She shook her head. "I promised her that her secret was safe with me."

Sterling narrowed his eyes. "We have to tell him right away."

"Why? She's terrified of being discovered. I only found out by accident."

Sterling's mouth flattened into a thin line. "Think about it Em. Paparazzi will be crawling all over town with McBride here. What's going to happen if they discover another superstar is in Prairie? Especially with the way she just disappeared? They'll go crazy. It will ruin the exhibition game. All the focus will be on Kaycee."

"But they won't be here at the ranch, will they?"

"One thing I've learned from Jason is to never underestimate the craziness of the paparazzi." Sterling stood and paced toward the door leading to his bedroom.

"Wait." Emma scrambled up, dropping the blanket and donning her clothes from where they were strewn across the floor. "You want to talk about this now?"

A moment later, Sterling returned in a pair of jeans, buttoning up a shirt. "The sooner we deal with this, the sooner we'll have a plan in place and can be prepared."

She liked this man of action side to him. And the way he looked out for the others on the ranch. Whatever his life in the Army had been, his calling now was clearly as foreman.

He paused at the door, extending his hand.

She studied him, then arched a brow. "We've graduated to holding hands in public now?"

"Those shoes may be sexy as fuck, but they're impractical."

Of course. Her heart squeezed a little tighter. "I'll be fine. I have great balance," she tossed back lightly.

"I don't want you twisting an ankle as we walk across the yard." He stretched his hand toward her. "Afraid of wagging tongues, Goldilocks?"

Her hand shot out to take his. "Never."

He shot her a triumphant grin as he took her hand, and damn if it didn't feel good, walking hand in hand across the yard with him, hand encased in his strong, warm grip. When they arrived at the farmhouse porch, he helped her up the steps then eyed her as he released her hand to knock on the door. His look taunted her, as if to say, *See? No harm, no foul.* When the reality hit her in that instant that she wanted more. Her stomach dropped like a stone. Wanting more from Sterling would result in heartbreak. Yet, she couldn't help it. She was so screwed.

Travis answered, a welcoming smile on his face. "Crashing our place for dinner?"

Emma opened her mouth to speak, but Sterling was in full-on foreman mode, taking control. "We have a problem. Can you call Kate and Cash over? We need to discuss the fundraiser."

Travis's gaze flicked between the two of them. "What's up?"

"Can we come in?" Sterling asked.

Travis opened the door wider, allowing them to pass. "Of course, of course. Have a seat. Let me get them over here."

The minutes ticked by uncomfortably as Sterling paced in front of the fireplace, and Travis's wife attempted to make small talk from the kitchen. Suddenly, Emma felt like this was all her fault. Like she was ruining everything by being here by having discovered Kate's secret. All her old insecurities came flooding back, building with each minute. By the time Kate and Cash rushed in the door, perspiration beaded at the base of her neck. This could ruin everything.

"What's going on?" Cash asked gruffly, surveying the room.

Emma shot an apologetic glance at Kate, who shook her

head, looking terrified. "Wait, Sterling. I don't think this is a good idea."

"What's a good idea?" Travis asked, looking more and more suspicious with each passing second.

"Umm, I wanted to give you an update about the concert," she said brightly, drawing a smile from somewhere around her toes. "I got the K-State Symphony to come down and play a concert of classical American music."

"Okay… And?"

Oh, this was bad. She was coming off looking inept. "Like a mini Symphony in the Flint Hills."

Sterling scowled at her. She glanced at Kate, who also scowled at her. But Sterling was right, they couldn't afford to have the paparazzi take them by surprise. Taking a deep breath, she crossed her fingers and spoke. "Kate. I know I'm betraying your confidence, and I'm so very sorry, but there are some new developments with the ranch that concern you."

"Will someone tell me what the fuck is going on?" Travis bit out.

Cash stepped forward, arms folded across his chest. "I should have told you sooner, Trav, but your ranch hand Kate, is actually Kaycee Starr."

Kate's face went white as she spun to Cash. "What? How did *you* know? No one knows." She glanced across to Emma. "Well, except Emma."

"I've known since the moment I laid eyes on you."

"How?"

Cash cleared his throat and shot a stern glance over to Travis. "We can discuss that later." Then he turned to Sterling. "But I want to know what's so important that you've found it necessary to blow her cover."

"Trace McBride," Sterling answered.

"*Trace McBride?* The actor?" Travis repeated incredulously.

Sterling nodded once. "He's coming to play for Army at the exhibition game."

Cash glowered.

"I see," answered Travis. "That's great news. But it does present some problems. We need to alert Weston. We'll have to bump up security. Does he have a place to stay?"

"Not yet."

"I'm sure he can stay at the hunting lodge," Emma piped up. "I'll check with Jamey and Brodie."

Travis nodded once, then cocked his head, studying Kate. "I wouldn't have known you from Adam. But having you here does present some issues." He furrowed his brows. "Can I still call you Kate?"

She nodded. "Please."

"For Kate's sake, and ours, it will be better if the press is camped out on the other side of town."

"But this will impact the activities we're planning at the ranch. What do we do for the poker tournament and the concert?" Emma asked before turning to Kate. "I still think Kaycee, *Kate,* should make a surprise appearance. The audience would be thrilled." Maybe Kate just needed convincing from more of them. Surely the young woman didn't believe in her heart of hearts that her career was over? Emma cringed inwardly. What must it be like to feel washed up at twenty-four? She didn't envy Kate one bit. But still… she had the voice of an angel, broken or not.

Kate's mouth flattened, and she shook her head. "I've already said no. As long as no one knows I'm here, I don't see that activity on the ranch would invade my privacy. But if you're worried… maybe it's time for me to go home." She spoke quietly, the weight of defeat permeating the room.

"You're welcome to stay as long as you like, Kate," Travis rushed. "You have a real gift with the horses. I'd hate to lose you."

Kate nodded. "I appreciate that. But I can't hide out here forever." Her eyes drifted to Cash, whose face was a mask. Then she looked at the three of them. "Please don't tell anyone I'm here," she pleaded. "I…" she took a ragged breath. "It would mean a lot to me to have these final weeks of privacy before I have to face the music." She smiled weakly at her joke.

Travis answered first. "Of course. We're in agreement. We keep this under wraps." His voice brooked no argument, not that any of them would betray her trust. Travis eyed each of them. "Kaycee's part of our ranch family now. We do for her as we'd do for any of us."

Emma loved how protective Travis was of his crew. Once again, it warmed her that she was able to help the ranch onto solid footing. "Kate, if it will make you more comfortable, I have additional copies of Royal Fountain's non-disclosures," said Emma. "They're the same form that I signed for you, and I can modify them for the ranch. We can sign them right now." She looked to Travis for confirmation. He nodded.

"I'd appreciate that," Kate answered after a moment, looking guilty. "I hope you understand. It's hard to know who to trust."

Emma dug into her bag and produced the forms. Taking them to the table, she made the necessary changes for the men, and then signed her initials. Poor girl. How awful to live in a fishbowl and not know who to trust. "Don't worry, Kate," she said with a reassuring smile, handing the young woman the completed forms. "Your secret's safe with us."

CHAPTER 21

S TERLING BROKE INTO a grin as Jason entered the small baggage claim area in Manhattan, then gave a surprised whoop as Macey and Sophie trailed after him.

"You son-of-a-gun." He clapped Jason's back as they embraced. Then he kneeled down, pulling Sophie into a hug, throat suddenly tight at the sight of Johnny's bright blue eyes staring up at him. "So good to see you, beanie."

"It was my idea," said Macey. "Sophie wanted to see her uncles." Her face twisted in pain. "And I did too. I need to start getting out." She took a deep breath. "And this seemed like the right place to make a start. I think Johnny would have–" her voice caught.

Sterling caught her arm. "I know. I think about it every day, Mace."

She brushed at her eyes.

"Well let's get you piled into the truck. Are you staying here in Manhattan?"

She shook her head. "We got the last room at someplace called *The Lodge at Steele Creek*?"

That name had Emma's handiwork all over it. "I bet that's the hunting lodge at Sinclaires'. That's where my–" he stopped. He'd nearly called Emma his girlfriend. Is that what she was? His belly clenched. He swallowed. "My friend Emma, she's been helping with publicity for the ranch. That's her family's place."

Jason shot him a look over Macey's head. One of those *you're full of shit, you asshole* looks. So what? If he introduced Emma as his girlfriend, it added a whole new layer of complication to their arrangement. He liked her. Loved spending time with her. But she wasn't his girlfriend. And he sure as hell wasn't going to flaunt a girlfriend in front of Macey. Not when she'd lost so much. It would be like pouring salt on an open wound. He shook his head. Jason glowered at him before turning to Macey. "Just a heads up, my friend Trace McBride is staying out there. He's arriving tonight."

Macey gasped. "*The* Trace McBride?"

Jason nodded. "He's our ace in the hole for beating Navy. And a friend of mine."

Macey socked him in the arm.

"*Ow.*" Jason grimaced, clutching his bicep. "What was that for?"

"That's for holding out on me. Since when did you start rubbing elbows with Trace McBride?"

"About a year ago. He came to the winery."

"Did Johnny know about this?"

The car fell silent. The heartbreak could be cut with a knife.

A small voice piped up from the back. "Daddy was sad for a long time."

Grief knifed through Sterling, and he tightened his grip on the steering wheel. He'd never get over the way grief just snuck up on him. In a comment, or a look. Sometimes without even prompting.

Macey sounded defeated when she spoke. "That's right, sweetie pie. Daddy was sad for a long time before he died."

"I miss Daddy," Sophie said with a tremor.

Macey turned, giving her daughter a reassuring pat. "I know. We all do. And it's okay to miss him."

Little Sophie's admission cut to the quick, and the remainder of the ride to the Sinclaire ranch was somber. "I'll grab the bags," Jason offered when they pulled into the drive in front of the hunting lodge and hopped out before Sterling could object.

"I'll grab Sophie," Sterling told Macey, coming around the front of the truck. "You go on in."

"Can we see the horsies Unka Stewing?" Sophie's chubby arms clasped his neck.

"I'm sure we can, poppet. If not here, then you can come to my ranch and I'll take you on a ride. How's that?" Sophie rewarded him with a beatific smile that looked so much like Johnny, it hurt. "C'mon punkin', let's get you inside to mama." He carried her around the car and through the open door of the lodge. To Sterling's surprise, Emma was waiting for them inside. Her face lit when she saw him, then fell, turning confused as she looked from him to Sophie, then to Macey.

Shit. Sterling's stomach sank like a stone. This looked bad. "Hi." He gave her a tentative smile.

"Hi." Her smile didn't reach her eyes and the cool mask of professionalism was firmly in place. She turned to Jason and offered a hand, and then to Macey. "I'm Emma Sinclaire. Welcome to the Lodge at Steele Creek. I'm thrilled you're here this weekend for our exhibition game. This ranch has been continuously run by my family since before the Civil War. I hope you'll find everything to your liking."

Macey extended her hand. "I'm Macey, and Sterling has my daughter, Sophie. We're friends of Jason and Sterling."

"Thank you for making the trip."

No one else likely noticed, but he did. The tight edge to her voice. The two slashes that appeared at the top of her nose. Shame burned in his chest. He should have told her. Explained about Johnny. But the times it had come up, he'd been too grief-stricken to talk about it. It had hurt too much.

"Is it okay for Sophie to have a cookie?" Emma asked Macey, and gestured to the credenza piled high with freshly baked snacks. "My sister-in-law is an excellent chef. She makes kitchen sink cookies filled with chocolate chips and much more, so they're a little bit nutritious. My nephew loves them."

Macey smiled at her, then opened her arms to receive Sophie "Would you like a cookie?"

Sophie burrowed into her mother, eyes wide and nodded.

He should say something. Explain. It all felt so awkward. But the words were stuck in his throat, and anything he said in front of Macey or Jason would pick at a scab that wasn't fully healed. Jason raised his eyebrows and knocked his chin in Emma's direction as she bent to retrieve a box from underneath the large farm table, then scowled when he shook his head.

"Sterling's told me all about your work for the fundraiser," Jason said, glaring daggers at him.

Emma turned and stood, a look of surprise on her face. "Really? Well, I hope it meets your expectations. I'm looking forward to the game tomorrow. And here." She held out a shirt. "This is your team shirt for tomorrow." She gave it to Jason, then turned to Macey. "I took the liberty of assuming you'd be supporting the Army if you're with these two?"

Macey gave her a pained smile. "Yes."

"And I have a child's small. It will be big for Sophie, but

you can knot it." She held the shirts out for Macey.

Macey's eyes filled with tears. He knew what she was thinking. He was thinking the same thing. Johnny should be here. The three of them should be doing this together, like they always did. "Jason?" Macey said thickly. "Can you keep an eye on Sophie? I need a minute. Please forgive me," she said to Emma as she hurried out the front door.

"Wait, Mace," Sterling called as he followed after her. He found her on the patio, leaning against the house, tears streaming from her face.

"Aww, hon." He pulled her into an embrace, and she shook in his arms.

"I can't do this," she sobbed. "I can't even talk to anyone without falling apart. How am I going to make it through this weekend?"

"You've got me and Jason. We'll do this together," he answered, his own voice tight with sorrow. "Johnny should be here. I hate that he's not. I don't know how he could do it."

Macey lifted her tear-stained face, and shook her head vehemently. "Don't say it. Don't. We have to move forward. All of us. You, me, Jason. And we have to keep the good parts of him alive for Sophie." She covered her face with her hands and breathed deeply. "Johnny wouldn't want us to be stuck like he was."

"It's one thing to say that. It's another thing to live it."

She wiped her eyes. "But we have to do it."

"But he's only been gone a handful of months, Mace."

"Three months and three weeks, to be exact." She speared him with a look. "I don't have the luxury of stopping life while I mourn. Sophie needs her one living parent to be fully present. And you owe it to your girlfriend–"

"She's not my girlfriend."

Macey held up a hand. "Don't say that. Jason filled me in on the plane ride. She sure sounds like your girlfriend, and Johnny would love that. He'd want that for you."

"But–"

"I'm so sorry to interrupt." Emma's voice sliced through him, cold as ice.

He whirled. Her eyes matched her voice. *Shit. Damn. Motherfucker.* Panic reeled through him. Had she overheard? Misconstrued? "Em–"

She held up a hand. "Save it." Then she turned to Macey, voice softening. "Jason brought me up to speed. I'm so very sorry for your loss."

Fuck.

Now he was in hot water. He should have been the one to tell Emma about Johnny. About Sophie and Macey. About their pact to always be there for Sophie. Instead, she heard it second-hand. For the second time in less than an hour, his chest burned. Everything he should have said flooded into his brain.

"Thank you," Macey murmured. "I'm sorry I made a scene. This is my first trip since, since…"

"I understand." Emma's voice was full of compassion. "Please make yourself at home while you're here. I have to run, but I'll look for you at the game tomorrow."

Hearing that finally spurred him to action. "Wait, Emma?"

She smiled tightly. Emma was never the one to make a scene. Even in high school, their battles had been private. She'd never once lost her cool when he'd taunted her publicly. But he recognized the steel in her eye. She was pissed as hell. And this time he deserved it. "I'm late for an appointment. Goodbye, Sterling." She disappeared around the corner.

His stomach pitched. She'd said those words plenty of times before, but never with the hard edge they were delivered with just now. Always with a smile, or a laugh, or a teasing note. Fear pooled in his gut. This was just a small misunderstanding, wasn't it? Not something to ditch him for? And if she ditched him, did that mean they *had* been dating and he'd been too stubborn to acknowledge it? He scrubbed a hand over his face trying to make sense of what in the hell had just happened.

Macey tsked. "Oooh. You're in trou-ble." Her voice pulled out the end sound.

He shook his head. "I don't understand what just happened."

Jason's prosthetic scraped against the patio. "Let me explain using small words." His voice held a hint of laughter. "You've been seeing Emma for three months–"

"Not seeing," he corrected. "And I was gone for a month."

Jason rolled his eyes and caught Macey's eye. "This is what I was talking about."

"Talking about what?"

"You have no right to sound offended when your head's stuck so far up your ass you can't even smell your own shit," Jason fired back. "Let me spell it out. You reconnected with Emma on New Year's Eve?"

He nodded.

"And in three months, it never occurred to you *even once* to mention that one of your best friends killed himself just before Christmas?"

Sterling winced. When Jason put it that way, he sounded like an ass.

"Do you have feelings for her?"

"Emma?" His voice caught in his throat. Like he was a teenager again struggling to pick a register.

Jason's face pulled tight. A sign that he was perilously close to losing his temper. "Yes, Emma. Who else?" Jason fisted his hands on his hips. "Here's the deal, asshole. If you have feelings for her, then you need to man up and apologize."

"Groveling works well," Macey added.

Sterling spun to her. "Not you too?"

She gave him an enigmatic smile. "Works wonders. If Johnny were here, he'd tell you how it worked for him."

"As I was saying," Jason continued. "If you have any feelings for Emma at all, then you need to go apologize. And if you're just an asshole." Jason spread his hands. "Then leave her the fuck alone."

For a stark moment, Sterling saw the two futures laid out side by side. One with Emma's smiling face, her laughter and wit. And their sizzling hot nights. The other? The bone aching loneliness like those first weeks at West Point. The cold look in her eyes when she'd left the Trading Post on a snowy New Year's Eve a few years later. The hollow spot in his chest that lately, hadn't felt so hollow.

He pinched the bridge of his nose. "I don't know what to do."

"Just say you're sorry, Sterling," said Macey gently. "If she's as nice as she seems, that's all she'll need to hear."

"It's not that simple."

Jason shook his head, clapping him on the shoulder. "It really is that simple. And we'll be right here for you the whole time. Go get 'em champ."

CHAPTER 22

H E'D TRIED HER phone three times throughout the afternoon. Radio silence.

It was his own fault, too. He'd completely mishandled her. Mishandled himself. But she could at least answer the phone. This time he'd leave a message. He hated leaving voice messages. But what else could he do if she refused to take his call? At least she'd know he was sorry.

If she listened to it.

He fought a wave of panic. She'd listen to it. She had to. He pressed call again. Still no answer. Only her professional greeting. Cool and calm and so unlike the firebrand she was when they were together. "Emma, Em. It's me. Sterling. Can we talk? Please? I owe you an apology. And I'd like the chance to make it in person. Any chance you can come over this evening? I'll make a fire and we can talk." Words piled up in his mouth. Important words. Scary words. Ready to tumble out if he let them. He ended the call and resumed his pacing.

The remainder of the afternoon crawled by. He saddled Bingo and rode the fence lines checking for broken spots. In the far north pasture, he pulled Bingo to a halt and slid off, fighting to pull a giant dead branch of red cedar off the fencing. Who knew what storm had carried it? But this was coming home as fuel for his fire pit. As he pulled it loose, the branch snapped back scraping across his cheek.

"Ouch. Goddammit."

Stomping back to Bingo, he grabbed a length of rope from inside the saddle bag that held his tools. He wound the rope around the base of the branch then walked back to Bingo and settled himself in the saddle. He dragged that damn branch all the way home. Past the tiny houses that would soon house their first group of veterans. Cash's and Kate's were now finished and stood apart from the others. The materials for the remaining homes sat on pallets in their respective areas, ready for the construction crews after the weekend's tournament.

He refrained from pulling his phone from his coat pocket. Emma hadn't called. He'd have felt the vibrations. Dropping the rope by his porch, he rode into the barn and took his time currying and caring for Bingo. "What is it with you ladies?" he asked as he scratched her cheek. "Can't figure any of you out."

Bingo dropped her head, pricking her ears forward, as if she had something to say. Giving her a final pat, he pulled out his phone. Even he knew enough to know never to apologize to a woman via text. But she gave him no choice. He wasn't about to let her go to bed angry. Or go to bed. He had better plans for her.

"You think make-up sex would help, Bingo?" Sterling grinned at the thought. Maybe he'd give her a bath. Better yet, a shower, where they both could enjoy the soap and the bubbles. His cock rose to half-mast just thinking about all the naughty and delightful things they could do underneath a spray of hot water. His thumb hovered over the keyboard, heart galloping. He started typing before he lost his nerve.

S: I don't want to ruin this weekend. Please come over so I can grovel in person?

He shoved the phone into his pocket and walked out of

the barn. If she was going to give him the cold shoulder, there was nothing he could do about it. As he stepped foot on the porch, his phone buzzed.

E: What time?

He gave a fist pump and fired off a quick reply.

S: Anytime you're ready to talk.

A moment later his phone buzzed again.

E: I'm wrapping up the final details for tomorrow's game. How about 7?

That sounded perfect. The sun would be setting about then, thanks to Daylight Savings. And he'd bet his last dollar she'd be hungry. She probably hadn't had a bite to eat all day. An idea formed in his head.

S: I'll throw some steaks on the grill.

E: Sounds great <3

His heart tripped at the emoji. She couldn't be that upset if she was adding heart emojis could she? Still. He wanted this night to be different. More... real. And he had just enough time to make it perfect.

When Emma's car crunched across the gravel two hours later, he was ready. His heartbeat quickened as her boots hit the steps to the door. He opened it before she had a chance to knock and the air whooshed out of his chest at the sight of her.

She'd changed her clothes. Her hair hung in loose waves down her shoulders, just the way he liked it. She'd put on a blue sweater with a wide vee neck that brought out her eyes and clung to her curves. From the looks of it, it was as soft as a baby's cheek. All the words he'd planned, the apology speech, the surprise on the back patio, all of it, flew from his head. "Come here," he said gruffly as he pulled her into an embrace and tenderly kissed her forehead. "I'm sorry. I've been an ass. Please accept my apology."

She gasped, eyes widening, making a sound of surprise in the back of her throat as she traced a finger over the scratch on his cheek. "Are you okay? What happened?"

"Just a scratch. And you look stunning."

"Thank you," she murmured.

"Come in? I have something to show you." He trailed a hand down her arm to lace his fingers with hers as he pulled her through the office and into the house. As he led her through the kitchen and out the back door, the smell of grilling meat wafted over them.

"Mmmm. I'm hungry," she said eagerly, then stopped as she took in the scene he'd set. "You bought *wine?*"

He stepped to the tiny table between two Adirondack chairs, and handed her a stemless globe filled with red liquid. "I thought it might be better for groveling."

She huffed out a laugh. "You didn't have to do this."

He absolutely had to do it. He needed to show her what he always seemed to mess up when words were involved. "I also noticed you only have wine at your apartment, even though you usually drink beer at the Trading Post."

She cocked her head, clearly surprised. "Beggars can't be choosers. And I like beer too."

"But you like wine better."

She nodded. "I do."

He gestured to the chair. "Sit. Steaks are almost done."

She sat, then swiveled to look up at him. "Why are you doing this?"

He leaned to place a kiss on her forehead. "Talk later. For now, just enjoy the fire." The difficult explanations would be easier on a full stomach in front of the fire. A knot of fear at the pain he knew was coming formed, sharp and tight in his chest. If he could enjoy the peace a little longer, he would. It was a perfect spring night. The air was soft, and smelled like fresh dirt and mown grass. But there was still enough chill in the air that a fire offered the perfect atmosphere. He plated the steaks, topped off their wine, and sat down next to her. Perching their plates on their knees, they ate in an easy silence as the night peepers began their chorus.

Emma put down her fork. "Thank you for dinner. Every part of it has been amazing. But you're making me nervous. All this…" she swept her hand around, "romance, is unlike you. Now will you tell me what's going on?" She braced an elbow on the arm, propping her chin on her hand. Eyes round and serious.

That she thought romance was unlike him, ate at him. Regret surged through him. He should have sent her flowers after he'd spent the weekend with her in Kansas City. Johnny had sent Macey flowers all the time. So much so, that he and Jason had teased him mercilessly. But their teasing hadn't been enough to stop him. He'd shrugged it off, smiled enigmatically, and said *just you wait*. And now Sterling knew what he meant by that. But the longing sparred with the fear. Twisted and danced inside him until he couldn't tell which was way up. What direction to move. It paralyzed him.

He stared into the fire. Tracing one flicker after another. Letting the movement hypnotize him. "Johnny was our best friend. He and Jason and I met during Beast, and we've been inseparable ever since. Johnny met Macey when we were Firsties, and right away, he knew she was the one. He came to us the next day and told us then he was going to marry her."

"That's sweet."

Sterling shook his head. "It really wasn't. Johnny was like a man possessed. He couldn't concentrate, talked of nothing but how amazing Macey was. Burned up the phone lines talking to her. He wrote her every day, and sent flowers. All the goddamned time. It was annoying as shit. But then we met her. And we understood why."

"She's lovely."

Sterling's head snapped up at the note of resignation in her voice. "She is lovely. The nicest person you'll ever meet. It's impossible not to love her." He reached out for Emma's hand. "But my interest in her is only brotherly." He stroked her soft skin with his thumb. "Jason and I made a pact to look after her, and to be the men in Sophie's life."

Emma made a sound in the back of her throat and dropped her head. "She's very lucky," she said thickly.

Sterling blew out a breath, as a sharp pain lodged in his sternum. "I'm doing a piss-poor job of explaining myself. We're not doing that because we think that's what Johnny would want us to do. Be there because he couldn't be. We're doing it – *I'm* doing it because I'm pissed as hell that Johnny's not here to finish what he started." His voice rose as the pent-up anger and hurt boiled over. "He fucking bailed on the two women he said he loved more than anything. He promised Macey forever, and brought a child into the world, and then he quit them." White hot anger blazed through him and he shook with the intensity of it. "He quit them," he said raggedly, then dropped his head into his hands. "I don't understand how he could quit them and leave us to pick up the pieces."

The pain hollowed his stomach, rising to close off his throat. He gulped in air, trying to regain some control. "He was one of my best friends." His vision blurred. "And I should have done more to help him." He sniffed hard through his nose, trying to grab back the emotions. Stuff them back inside. But they were having none of that. "I don't understand how he could leave his wife and daughter. How he could give up on them. On us. Me and Jason."

He stood, pacing around the fire. "We had a pact." He kicked a rock at the edge of the fire pit. "We were in this together to the very end." Hot tears wet his eyes and he kicked the stone again.

"Sterling?"

He heard the concern in her voice, but he was on a roll, anger spewing out of him with volcanic force. He stalked back to where she was perched on the chair and he bent over the chair next to her. "And you want to know why I didn't tell you? Why I never brought it up?" He dragged the chair out of the circle of warmth and threw it into the yard. "Because I'm a *man.*" He followed the chair and gave it a mighty kick, splintering the back. He dimly registered a squeak from Emma but he'd unleashed the fury, letting it take over. "I'm a goddamned soldier and we *don't. Fucking. Cry.*" He punctuated each word with another kick, destroying the chair. His voice was raw. Gravelly. "We soldier on and we get the fucking job done *no matter what.*"

He turned, and seeing tear-stained cheeks glistening in the firelight, turned away again. "And *I. Can't. Handle this,*" he bellowed, throat on fire. His knees gave way and he roared to the sky. "Why'd you quit us Johnny? What gave you the right?" He fell forward, pounding his palm into the ground, not feeling the sharp pebbles biting his skin. "Fuck you, man," he sobbed as the tears erupted. His lungs burned. "Fuck you," he barked, continuing to pound the dirt.

And then her hands on his shoulders. "Hush, Sterling. It's okay. It's going to be okay."

"It's not," he bawled. "What if I turn into him? What if I go off the rails and I do what he did?" He shook his head, leaning back on his heels.

Her hand stayed on his back, rubbing in concentric circles. "You're not going to. You're not Johnny."

"I don't believe that." He wiped his face on his arm. Calm slowly seeping in where the anger had burned.

Emma's voice acted like a cooling balm. "I remember feeling so angry when my father died. And he was horrible. My brothers don't even refer to him as dad."

Sterling didn't remember much about Jake Sinclaire. They'd been freshman when he'd died, and he'd been too caught up in girls and football to pay much attention to the gossip his parents discussed. "I was angry for how my mother kept giving him chances he didn't deserve. Angry when he left us. Angry that my mother got sick and left us too, after the hard life she'd had. I was so mad at the injustice of it all, I vowed I'd never be like either of them. And if you don't want to end up like Johnny, you won't."

"It's not that simple, Emma. You know that."

She stood and reached for a section of the splintered chair. Then she walked to the fire and tossed it on the flames. The fire hissed and sprang higher in a shower of sparks.

"There are no guarantees in life. I understand that." She turned and looked at him full-on. "But I'd never bet against you, Sterling. Not in a million years."

CHAPTER 23

S HE LOOKED LIKE some sort of avenging angel, glowing orange backlit by the fire, and radiating such fierce conviction it constricted his throat. Wielding absolution with one hand and terror with the other. Her voice shook when she spoke. "You're *nothing* like Johnny, Sterling. Nothing."

Her words laid him bare. Sliced through his armor and exposed his vulnerable underbelly. She could see his deepest fears. His darkest secrets. Rising to his feet, he stumbled toward her, catching her in a tight embrace, holding on for dear life. "I need you, Emma." He needed all of her. Her softness to absorb his hardness. Her fierce strength. Her sweetness that tasted like forever.

Bending, he swept her legs up and turned, carrying her into the house. Kicking shut the back door, he swiftly carried her through the house, setting her down when he reached his bedroom. Her hand reached out for the light switch, but he caught it, shaking his head. "I want to see you," he said roughly as he toed off his boots, not caring where he flung them.

He registered the thud of her boots joining his somewhere on the floor. He tilted her chin and claimed her mouth with bruising intensity, tongue sweeping into her sweet mouth faintly tasting of wine, and plundering her recesses. She seemed to recognize this deep, primal need to possess her entirely and she moaned as he deepened the kiss, melting into him and kissing him back with equal passion.

Her hands were everywhere. Alternately clutching his shoulders, then spearing through his hair, pulling him closer. She grabbed at the buttons on his shirt, and mouth still on hers, he covered her hands and jerked, popping the buttons all the way down. Lust pounded in his veins as he sought the edge of her sweater and yanked it up, only stopping his assault on her mouth to pull the sweater over his head.

They came at each other again. So quickly they bumped noses, teeth. She came alive at his touch, skin heating under his fingers, moaning in the back of her throat. He palmed her breast, seeking her nipple through the fabric of her bra. With a noise, she reached behind herself and released the clasp, shrugging her shoulders to fling it across the room. "Touch me," she said with a sigh. "Make me yours."

He cupped her breasts, heavy and full, teasing her nipples into tight peaks, his cock jerking against his zipper with each sigh, each cry. Rolling them between his fingers, he gave a little tug and she arched, exposing the creamy column of her neck. He tongued the corded length, laying a nip at her collarbone. Her arousal rose from her, mingling with her perfume. A heady drug that had his head spinning as he tasted her skin. "Yessss," she hissed. "Do it again."

He walked her back until they hit the edge of the bed, and she sat, hands moving to his waistband, but he moved out of reach, dropping to his knees, fingers working the clasp of her jeans. As soon as the zipper was down she arched her hips and hooking his fingers through the lace of her panties, dragged everything off, exposing her completely.

His breath caught in his chest. "So beautiful," he murmured as he slowly inspected her. "So perfect." From the red mark where he'd nipped her collarbone, to her dusky puckered nipples, to the pale expanse of her torso, and the soft swell of her belly. She was everything he'd dreamed. He drew a finger from the base of her throat, down the valley between her breasts, across her silken skin, stopping at her mound. With a mewling cry, she flexed her hips, pushing her pubic bone into him, a silent pleading for more.

His heart raced, pounding against his ribs, as he forced himself to slow down. His breath came in harsh rasps. Adrenaline surged through him, sharpening his focus. A pale fuzz barely covered her pussy. And he stroked over the soft thatch, touching lightly as her hips rolled. He groaned as he slipped a finger between her swollen pussy lips into her slick heat. She cried out at his touch, a shiver running through her body. With his thumb, he found her clit and worked it in a circle, as he pumped a second finger into her channel.

She clutched the bed, writhing.

"Come for me, baby."

Her eyes flew open. "On your cock," she ground out. "I want to come with you."

Fuck.

Her gaze was wild, untamed. As lust-crazed as he was, and it burned straight through to his soul. He slipped his hand from her, keeping her gaze while he slowly licked his fingers, lapping up her sweetness like she was water in the desert. In one swift move, he dropped his pants, freeing his cock. She scrambled back, making room for him, and he braced his hands on either side of her head, looming over her.

"You want my cock?" he rasped. "Tell me again how much you want my cock."

Lust flamed in her eyes and she nodded. "I want all of you."

But there was so much more in her gaze than lust.

His heart cracked open. This was too much. It felt too big. Like he was being turned inside out and shoved through a pinhole all at once. He made a choked sound as she moved under him, and then he slid home. Buried himself balls deep in her sweetness.

Her hand cupped his cheek. "Sterling," she breathed out on the softest sigh. He answered her with a thrust of his hips, and she arched to meet him. "I'm right here," she murmured as she captured his gaze. "I'm right here."

He wanted to hide, but she'd broken through every last defense and he was bare before her as they rocked together. The fire in her eyes captured him like a tractor beam, and he couldn't look away. It kept his soul from shattering into a million pieces. Heat raced up the back of his legs in a shower of sparks. His balls tightened with a heavy ache as she moved with him in a primitive dance that he was powerless to stop. The only thing he could do was ride the wave between them. "Emma," he choked out as hot emotion ran like lava through his veins. "Oh God, Emma," he cried out as his orgasm ripped through him, spotting his vision.

She spasmed around him as she followed him over the edge, crying out, "I'm right here, Sterling. Not going anywhere." Her eyes were wet with tears.

He kissed her, continuing to move. First her temples, salty and wet. Then her cheeks, and at last, coming home to her soft lips. He couldn't speak. Words weren't big enough or adequate enough. He lifted his head, staring down at her, memorizing the pale freckles across her nose, the creases at the corner of her eyes, the flush of her cheek, rosy from their lovemaking.

Her eyes flicked to his, warm and shining, and she parted

her lips to speak. He kissed her again, stopping her. If either of them spoke, the spell would be broken, and he wanted this perfect moment to go on and on. To hold everything else at bay. Because he couldn't handle the shitstorm of feelings about to crash over him. He rolled them onto their sides, and buried his face in her neck, breathing her in.

"Sterling?" her voice was muffled in his shoulder.

He tightened his embrace. "Shh. Let me just hold you."

CHAPTER 24

SUNLIGHT STREAMED THROUGH the blinds, and she reached across the bed, coming fully awake when her hand found only cool sheets. She sat, rubbing her eyes, and found Sterling, fully dressed, sitting in the chair across from the bed, head bent and resting his elbows on his knees. Her stomach dropped.

"Everything okay?" He raised his head. Everything was most certainly *not* okay. His eyes had the look of a haunted man. "Sterling?" She scrambled out of bed, not caring she was stark naked. "What is it? Did something happen?"

She reached for him, but he shrugged her away. "You need to go," he said woodenly.

Her blood ran cold. "Wait. What? What do you mean?"

"God help me, Em. I love being with you," he rasped.

Oh, God. *OhGodOhGodOhGodOhGod. Nooooo.* She recognized that tone of voice. But it didn't make sense. Not after what they'd shared the night before. She was falling in love with him. She'd talked about her parents. She *never* talked about her parents with anyone. Not even her brothers. "I don't understand." But the sick feeling in her stomach said she understood all too well what was coming.

He looked at her, eyes dull. Face pulled tight. "You were right about there being no guarantees. I was up all night thinking about it. Watching you sleep. I was a monster last night."

"You were angry and hurting." She'd seen far worse in her own home. Last night had been an uncharacteristic outburst of grief. Nothing more.

"You don't know that," he said harshly. "*I* don't know that. What if the next time I throw something at you? Or worse?"

Panic swirled up through her body, making everything pass in slow motion. "I *know* you. That's not who you are. You're not a violent person. Neither are your parents. I've never seen you start a fight. Or intimidate or disrespect anyone. You've never been anything but a gentleman."

He lifted his head back. "Ha."

"You're grieving, Sterling. Grief takes time. But it's not a reason to walk away from love."

His eyes bored into her, icy and wild. "Is that what you think this is?"

Her breath caught in her chest. Last night? She'd have said yes. The second she'd awakened? Same. But now? She was packing up the private Emma and hiding her behind a wall, too scared to say what she wanted for fear of what he might say. "I think it could be," she said slowly.

"This isn't love," he said harshly. "It's chemistry. It's fucking."

His words sliced to her core. Right through her defensive walls to the very heart of her. "I know why you're doing this," she articulated when she could find her voice again. "I know why you're pushing me away. And you don't need to."

"You don't know what I need," he growled.

A flame sparked to life in her chest. "What you need," she snapped back, "is a slap upside the head."

He glared at her. "Is that so?"

"Yes. It is. And I want a legitimate reason from you as to why you're telling me to leave." She wasn't going to let him run away from this. Not after last night.

He scrubbed a hand over his face, suddenly looking exhausted. "We've been over this. I don't know how else to spell it out."

"Well you better try real hard, mister." Anger fisted in her chest. Clearing her head, sharpening her tongue.

"Fine." He stood and tossed her sweater on the bed. "Get dressed."

She stood, too. "No. If you're going to send me away. Then you're going to see what you're giving up on." She'd use every weapon at her disposal this morning.

"I'm not giving up on anything. There was never anything *to* give up on."

She arched a brow. "Is that so? Nothing?"

He tossed her pants on the bed, eyes raking over her. Her hopes rose. There was a flicker of heat there. Of longing. "Nothing."

"Liar." Her throat tightened as her mind reeled. Why was he doing this? This didn't make sense. "I want one good reason from you why I should walk out of here."

"Fine," he bit out, squeezing his hips. "I'm not going to break you or anyone else the way Johnny broke Mace."

"That's a load of crap, Sterling. How do you know sending me away right now won't break me?"

His head whipped up, eyes boring into her. At least that got his attention. "You don't love me." His voice was clipped. Dry. Hopeless.

Her heart slammed into her throat, and she stood on the edge of a chasm. Terrified to jump, yet knowing it was the only way across the gulf between them. "What if I did?" she whispered thickly.

He let out a harsh sigh. "Then I'd tell you you're barking up the wrong tree, because I can never be the man you deserve."

She shut her eyes, willing the tears back into her skull. "What if you're the man I want?"

"I'd tell you you're a fool," he rasped, raking a hand over his head and regarding her with terrible eyes. "Because." He shuddered and gulped. "Because I don't want you."

Emma stopped breathing. In a flash as searing and rapid as a lightning bolt tearing through a tree, his words cleaved her heart in two. Only the thunder was the roar of her blood in her ears. "You don't mean that," she said, putting as much iron into her words as she could muster. "Look me in the eye and tell me again that you don't want me, that everything between us was all an act."

She swallowed when he looked at her, the unbending steel in his eyes, and she knew he'd do it. He'd tell her. This was Sterling the warrior. Sterling the soldier with a mission to complete. And his mission was to purge her from his life. She swallowed down the sob that threatened to shred her voice.

His words were succinct. As sharp as glass. "I. Don't. Want. You."

Only through sheer will, was she able to keep her spine ramrod straight and not collapse in a heap. "I feel sorry for you Sterling. I really do. That you have chosen loneliness and despair over the possibility of love." She sniffed, gathering her anger around her like a cloak. "Because, in the end, that's all we have. What's most important is our ability to give and receive love. It's the only thing that separates us from the animals, and it's the only glimpse we get of heaven." She glowered at him, drawing on every last bit of strength she had.

"You're not half the man I thought you were." She swept from the room, keeping her head high, snagging the blanket from the couch and wrapping it around her like a toga as she marched through the office and to her car, offering a silent plea to the universe to spare her the humiliation of running into anyone.

CHAPTER 25

S OMEHOW SHE MADE it back to the ranch without running the car into a ditch, and managed to make it to her bedroom without running into anyone. A small miracle in a house filled to the brim for the big game.

In a fog, she pulled on her favorite jeans and one of the exhibition tees she'd had printed for the game.

She's not my girlfriend.

I. Don't. Want. You.

The words she'd overheard and the words he'd flung at her materialized in her head. How could she have been such a fool? He hadn't changed. He was as capricious as he'd ever been. A tear squeezed out of her eye and her hands shook as she buttoned up the exhibition jersey with the Kansas City Kings logo. For a split second, she contemplated wearing the Navy cap. But then her shoulders sagged. What would that prove?

Nothing.

And for the first time, she didn't want to act like everything was okay. That nothing affected her. Let Sterling see the fallout from his stubbornness. From his stupidity. At least she was ready for today. It turned out to have been a good thing that she'd taken care of nearly all the details yesterday, while she had a brain. She could get through the next six hours. It would suck, but she could do it. Then she could go home to

Kansas City and lick her wounds in peace. By the time she returned to Prairie to wrap up work on the poker tournament and concert, she'd be good as new. She'd make sure of it.

She blinked hard, shoving back the wave of nausea that threatened to turn her stomach inside out.

Heck, maybe she'd even take a trip to New York City to see her fellow Athena Scholar sisters. They were always bugging her to come visit. She grabbed her phone and typed a note to herself to look into that as soon as she was home.

Pinching some color into her cheeks, she glanced into the mirror and practiced smiling. She looked on the verge of tears. That wouldn't do. Not with so many big names descending on Prairie. She'd have to rely on the cover of sunglasses. At least everything was taking place outside.

Twisting her hair into a low bun and opting for no baseball cap, she rolled her shoulders back and left for town. She wasn't on the fast track to the corner office at Royal Fountain because she took things lying down. No sirree. She'd overcome obstacles before. Sterling was just another obstacle. But even a personal pep-talk couldn't spare her from the piercing in her heart as the thought entered her head. Filling her lungs and blowing out slowly, she blinked back tears. She could do it. She could look at him without falling to pieces. Her mother had endured worse, and never cracked... in public.

Emma pulled into the high school parking lot just ahead of the Kings' team bus. Out of the corner of her eye, she saw Travis, Weston, and Cash. And across the lot Sterling stood huddled next to Jason with Trace McBride. Even with sunglasses on, it was obviously him. Rounding out the group was Macey holding little Sophie. Her heart flip-flopped as she quickly looked away. Grabbing a clipboard from her bag on the seat, she hopped out of the car, smile firmly in place when the bus door opened and Alex Jordan hopped out. He caught her in a bear hug and swung her around.

"You look fabulous, Emma. Gorgeous as ever."

A little ego fluff wouldn't hurt at all today. "You look pretty good yourself." She patted his broad chest. "The exhibition jerseys look fantastic. You all ready?"

He nodded. "You've met Marki and Rock before, but let me introduce the rest of the guys."

One by one, she met the team and waved Travis and the others over. "Alex, let me introduce to you the founder of Resolution Ranch, Travis Kincaid."

Travis stepped up, offering his hand with an easy smile. "It's an honor to meet you. Thank you so much for all you're doing for us."

"The honor is ours. Believe me. My cousin is still at Walter Reed, or he'd be here too. We need more organizations like yours, doing tangible, meaningful work with veterans."

"You're helping us get started on the right foot," Travis answered. "And let me know when your cousin is ready to join us. We'll keep a space for him."

Emma looked at the clock she'd attached to the clipboard. "We have an hour until the official event. Our diner won't be up and running until May 1ˢᵗ, but a little birdie told me there's special breakfast and orange juice waiting for all the players over at the food truck. Why don't we head that direction? Once you've eaten, you can toss the ball before we have the official autograph session."

"I'll take them over," Travis offered.

"Sounds great." Alex gave her a side hug and took off after Travis.

Sensing eyes on her, Emma turned her head to catch

Sterling shooting daggers at Alex's back. She pushed away a hysterical sob. He'd given up all right to be jealous this morning. She'd done nothing to be ashamed of. Nothing that she wouldn't have done if Sterling was right by her side and things had gone differently. "How is everyone this morning?" she forced herself to say brightly as the quartet passed.

Jason cocked his head at her, looking at her quizzically. "Great. Slept like a baby."

"Glad to hear it." Her voice felt brittle. Thin. Sterling focused on something far away, barely acknowledging her. Thank God for her sunglasses. She turned to the man in sunglasses. He was shorter than she'd imagined. Barely six feet by her estimation, and trim, but more slender than Sterling. He had the air of a man who lived an easy life. She extended her hand. "And you must be Trace? Thank you so much for joining us today. It means so much that you want to help our cause.

He flashed her a brilliant white smile. "Happy to help. Jason has become a good friend of mine, and anytime I can use my reputation to give back, I'm happy."

His words rang true, and Emma relaxed a fraction. "I hope you enjoy yourself this weekend."

He gave her hand a final squeeze. "I plan on it. I love the lodge. I'd love to come back another time. Get to know the area."

Excitement flushed her cheeks. "That's wonderful. I'm sure Brodie and Jamey would be thrilled to have you."

"Maybe you could show me around."

Was he flirting? A flash of anger burned through her. She should flirt back. Let Sterling see what he was missing. She flicked a quick glance at Sterling. He stood stony-faced, eyes fixed on the horizon. Not even looking at her. It was like she no longer existed. Emma's stomach hollowed. She wanted to scream. Hit him, pound on his chest until he came to his senses. But if she did that, she'd be as weak as her mother. Letting him go was her only choice, even though the thought of it took her breath away. She let out a little laugh, shaking her head. "Sorry. I no longer live at the ranch. But I'm sure we can find someone if you're interested."

Jason clapped Trace on the back. "Come on, let's get breakfast. The paparazzi are starting to circle like sharks. We've got to keep moving. You coming too, Emma?"

She shook her head, and turned for her car. "No. I've a few last-minute items to take care of before the game starts."

Autopilot kicked on, and she pushed her feelings aside as she slipped into event mode. By the time the team and visiting veterans trickled back, everything was set. From the banner for the photo-ops to the table showing off raffle prizes, every detail on her pages of lists had been checked off. She approached a group of photographers dragging big telephoto lenses, video cameras and microphones. These guys made her skin crawl. They embodied the worst of the press, and she'd do what she could to mitigate their presence today. "Good morning, gentlemen. I'm Emma Sinclaire. I'm handling media for this event."

One burly photographer, smelling of cigarettes, stepped forward. "We have every right to be here."

"No one's disputing that. But I want to make sure *everyone* has a pleasant time today," she said firmly. "First and foremost, this is a fundraiser for an organization helping injured veterans. Everyone here today has given money to support the work of Resolution Ranch." She pulled off her sunglasses, looking each of the slime bags in the eye. Today of all days, she was in no mood to take their crap. "Trace

McBride and the Kansas City Kings are here for the veterans, their families, and the fans who have donated to Resolution Ranch. You do not have the right to interrupt them when they are speaking to the public. You must maintain a respectful distance and respect their desire for privacy. You may not take pictures of minors, and you must ask permission to take a photo of any non-celebrity. Do I make myself clear?"

A couple photographers grumbled, but mostly they nodded their assent. "Of course, if you feel so inspired to make a donation to the ranch, you are welcome to do so. We would welcome your support." She gave them a cold smile and turned for the ball field.

"Hey, Goldilocks," a voice behind her called.

Whirling, she sought the owner of the voice. When she made eye-contact with him, instinctively, she knew he was the kind of sleaze bag who'd sell out his grandmother. She marched right up to him. "I have a name. Use it. Or I'll be happy to have security invite you to find another celebrity to stalk."

A few of the men on either side of him snickered, and she raked her gaze imperiously over the lot of them. "Any other questions?" she snapped. "Good." She replaced her sunglasses and marched back to where the players were grouped together, adrenaline pumping. It might be the only armor she had today, but she'd use it.

Alex flashed her a look of concern. "You okay? You look like you're ready to rip someone's balls off."

"I'm fine. I don't know how you guys do it, living in a fishbowl."

He grinned at her. "That's why they pay us the big bucks."

"I guess so. Everyone ready?"

After the high school choir sang the national anthem, Emma introduced the line-up and Travis. "Be generous today, ladies and gentlemen. We have the opportunity to make a big difference in the lives of men and women who've put their lives on the line for us. Please give a big thank you to our servicemen and women." She loved that Cassidy Grace was playing for the Army side. Sneaking a look at Sterling, even he wore a smile as the crowd jumped to their feet. And Jason Case wasn't the only veteran playing with a prosthetic. A man playing for Navy had a prosthetic arm. According to a very pregnant Elaine, some of the players today would be returning in a month to become the first class of Resolution Ranch Veterans. Six weeks of horse training, farrier and farm work, concluded by a six-hundred-mile trek following the Santa Fe trail. At one point, she'd considered volunteering to be trail support, but no more. The proximity to Sterling would be too painful.

The game started off with Weston Tucker first at bat for Navy. *Crack.* On the second pitch, he sent a ball flying over the fence. Score one for Navy, and with it came the salty talk.

The fans loved it, responding with their own Army vs. Navy cheers. In spite of the black cloud and the beginnings of a migraine hanging over her, it cheered her to see so many people she loved wearing smiles, relaxing, and obviously having a good time.

By the fourth inning, the teams were tied two-two with Army at bat, zero outs, and a runner at second. Sterling walked up to bat, making a show of getting ready to swing as Salvador Márquez, "Marki", gave him pointers from his position as catcher.

Forgetting herself, she yelled as Sterling took a swing and made contact with the ball sending it into left field. "Go, go, go!" she screamed as Sterling rounded first base and held up at second. Score another for Army.

"Sure you don't want to double down, Frogman?" Sterling hollered at Travis, who had moved to play outfield.

Travis threw his head back in a hearty laugh. "Game ain't over yet, my friend. Just remember who's come out on top fifteen of the last sixteen years. Navy *always* beats Army."

The crowd and the pros loved the banter between the two teams. They were evenly matched, and it made for exciting ball. During the seventh inning stretch, Emma made a final plea. "Don't forget, Trace McBride is over at the raffle table autographing raffle tickets and spreading a little luck of the Irish. After the game, the players and veterans will be around to sign autographs and take pictures. Then we'll look forward to seeing you out on the ranch on May 1st for high stakes poker, a concert and fireworks. Thanks again for supporting our veterans."

The rest of the game flew by in a blur, and the knot of tension screaming between Emma's shoulder blades only released when the bus pulled away. All she wanted was to drive home and curl up under a blanket and sleep for a week. But at least it was over. And she had a month to gear up for the final fundraiser. After that, she'd refer Travis to a coworker. One of the junior execs would hop all over this. She slipped into the driver's seat, pressing her fingers to her temples trying to ease the band of pain squeezing her head. But it was only when she glanced over to where she'd left her bag with her phone and iPad on the passenger seat that the jewel in the crown of this craptastic day winked up at her. Some asshole had stolen her bag.

CHAPTER 26

J ASON STROLLED INTO the Foreman's office ahead of
Sterling. "Emma joining us for dinner?"

Following him, Sterling grunted.

"I take it that's a no?" Jason walked through the living
area, past the place where the vision of Emma in red stilettos
and lacy lingerie was imprinted on Sterling's brain, past the
arm of the couch he'd bent her over and said every dirty thing
she'd asked him to while fucking her until they both
collapsed, and out onto the deck where the splintered remains
of the Adirondack chair were scattered. Jason stopped and
whistled, surveying the scene, then gave him a flinty stare. "I
take it you fucked up the apology?"

Sterling squirmed and shoved his hands in his pockets. "I
don't want to talk about it." *You're not half the man I thought
you were.* Didn't she realize he was saving her from future
despair? Sure, it might hurt now. But not like it would if
they'd... if they'd married and had children.

The image of Emma holding her nephew swam before
him. The way she bent to say hello to Sophie. She'd make a
great mother. For someone else. So why did it feel like he was
being skinned alive?

Jason's voice was as hard as his eyes. "Spill."

He shook his head, and picked up a piece of the broken
chair, chucking it as far as he could. "I said I don't want to

talk about it."

"And I'm not leaving until you do." Jason's voice rose. "You were a douchebag today. Barely civil to Alex Jordan and you about ripped Trace's head off when he commented about Emma. Something happened and you're going to fucking spill even if I have to beat it out of you."

Sterling glared at his best friend. "You wouldn't."

Jason crossed his arms, a muscle twitching high on his cheek. "Don't test me."

He glowered at Jason for a long moment. He could walk away, but Jason would take him down. He'd seen him take on his brothers before. The Case men weren't afraid to use their fists when talking failed. But he wasn't going to punch the man he loved like a brother. No fucking way.

The fight left him and he flopped into the remaining Adirondack chair, dropping his head into his hands. He swore he could still detect the lingering aroma of Emma's perfume. "I fell apart last night," he mumbled.

Jason's prosthetic scraped against the brick. "Come again?"

"I fell apart last night," he snapped. "I fucking lost it in front of Emma. I kicked the chair. I sobbed like a baby. The whole nine yards."

"And?"

"And what?" his voice cracked. "That's bad enough."

"Not bad enough for you to be an asshole today. What happened between you and Emma?"

Guilt beaded at his neck, like a string of pearls, one by one squeezing off his air. He shook his head.

"Did she laugh?"

"No."

"Did she call you a pussy?"

"No."

"Did she tell you to man up?" She'd definitely done that, but not in the context Jason implied. "What did she do?"

Sterling rubbed his face. "Anyone tell you that you should've been a JAG lawyer?"

Jason laughed dryly. "Once or twice. Answer my question."

"She was great. She was everything."

"So you found it necessary to be an asshat to the woman you've been crazy about for years? What the fuck for?"

"You seriously have to ask?" Sterling looked at Jason incredulously. Why was he being so obtuse? The answer was as plain as the nose on his face.

"Yes. I do," Jason bit out, clearly at the end of his patience. "Because I seriously want to punch your lights out, and unless you give me good reason not to, someone needs to woodshed your ass."

Sterling stood. "Look at Macey." He pointed in the direction of the Sinclaire Ranch. "You wanna know why I told Emma to go away? Take a good fucking look at Macey. She's a wreck, and she has to raise Sophie all alone."

"Not alone. She has us."

"From a distance. And you know what I mean. I'm not going to do to Emma what Johnny did to Macey. No fucking way."

"So you quit her now as opposed to later."

"Yeah." He hated that Jason put it that way.

"Broke her heart now, instead of maybe breaking it someday."

"I didn't break her heart," Sterling said defiantly. He couldn't break her heart. She didn't love him. Nevertheless, a tendril of doubt crept into his thoughts.

"Did you even look at her once today? She looked like someone had died."

His neck burned. "I didn't need to look at her. Alex Jordan and Trace were all over her."

Jason's fist connected with his jaw in a flash of ear-ringing pain. Sterling staggered back. "*OW*. What in the hell was that for?"

Jason shook out his hand and paced the length of the patio. "You've had that coming all day, dumbass. Do I have your attention now?"

Sterling nodded once.

"To recap. You had Emma over last night with the intention of apologizing. Which you did... sort-of. It ended with you having a breakdown, and Emma telling you that it was okay. That you were okay."

"But I'm not okay."

"Shut-up." Jason resumed his pacing. "Then at some point this morning, you told her to get lost out of some misguided idea that you were sparing her from future pain."

Sterling studied his shoes.

"Dude. That is some kind of fucked-up. I hope Travis has a shrink because, man, you need some serious couch time."

Shame licked up his spine.

Jason's voice softened a fraction. "Have you talked to anyone about Johnny's death? Besides me?"

"My parents."

"Someone who has experience dealing with grief? A pastor? A shrink? A superior officer?"

"Like I'd talk to an S.O. after my injury? They said I wasn't fit for the Rangers anymore."

"You're not, and you know it." He gestured to his leg. "I'm not either. Shit happens. Are you going to move on or stay stuck?"

Sterling fisted his hands on his hips. "God you sound just like Emma."

Jason laughed harshly. "Then you really are an idiot and I like her even more. You know why Johnny went the way he did? He stayed stuck. He bottled it up and didn't talk to anyone. Not even Macey. You don't want to be like Johnny? Start talking. With me, with Emma if she'll ever speak to you again, with Macey or Travis or the other guys at the ranch. Or a shrink. *Someone.* Because I guarandamntee you that if you stay stuck… If you don't move forward… I'm gonna be throwing dirt on your coffin, too."

CHAPTER 27

E MMA PUSHED BACK from her desk with a groan. Fresh air. Fresh air would clear her head. Help her chase the cobwebs away so she could think. Grabbing her sweater, she made her way to the rooftop garden that sat atop Royal Fountain's building at Sixteenth and Main.

The week had crawled by, punctuated only by the hassle of purchasing a new phone, and remotely shutting off the stolen devices. Wherever they were now, they'd be nothing more than paperweights. The worst? The most heart-wrenching confirmation that Sterling meant every word he'd spoken to her? His silence.

Emma sighed heavily as she pushed through the doors and into the late morning sun. The spring air was ripe with possibility. A riot of color exploded from several large planters near the balcony. Hyacinths, tulips, and a few late daffodils remained, scattered among the Japanese maples and weeping cherries. Dropping to a bench in her favorite corner, she leaned her head back and let the sun kiss her face. Maybe if she stayed here long enough the ice cube that had taken up residence in her chest would melt.

Sleep pulled at her. She'd forced herself into a brutal schedule of sixteen-hour days, working round the clock to catch up with clients and projects she'd neglected over the last three months while she'd devoted her energy to Resolution

Ranch. She should feel proud that her efforts, combined with Sterling's, were closing in on the half-million-dollar mark. Instead, she ached.

Her muscles ached when she dragged herself out of bed in the mornings, groggy from poor sleep. Her face ached from smiling. She'd avoided talking to her family because she couldn't talk about the ranch without spilling her guts, and the last thing she wanted was for her brothers to "have a talk" with Sterling. She couldn't make him want her. Even now, the vision of his face, tight and cold, brought tears to her eyes. He'd been so swift, so unequivocal in his rejection. "Better to have loved and lost than never loved at all," she muttered to herself. Stupid axiom. Tennyson had obviously never had his heart stomped to pieces.

Lying there, she let her mind wander over the details of the upcoming concert. Sound system rental. Check. Backstage and VIP tents reserved. Check. Security. Check.

If the past weekend was any indication, security wouldn't be an issue for the upcoming concert. Weston had stepped up police presence at key points, and many of the guys she'd gone to high school with had volunteered for security detail. Most had already volunteered to help with the next event.

The raffle prizes would be delivered the day before the concert, and Jamey and Dottie were taking care of food. The only details left involved the poker tournament and Sterling had volunteered to coordinate most of that. She'd have to call him to check in at some point, but she could wait. Let her heart heal a bit longer before she heard his voice again.

The only thing not checked off her mental list was confirming final contributions from her big donors, and she could take care of that this afternoon. Maybe she needed to book that trip back to New York now. Why wait until after the final fundraiser? A weekend of pampering, girl-talk, and Cosmos would be just what her bruised heart needed. She could probably nab a three o'clock flight and be back Monday afternoon. She reached for her phone, then remembered she left it downstairs.

Refreshed from the sunlight and the possibility of a diversion, she hurried back to her office. When the elevator doors opened, Gina, her assistant, rushed in, bringing an air of panic. "*Ohmygosh* I'm so glad I found you. I don't know what's going on, but your phone has been lighting up like a Christmas tree, and Mr. Prince came looking for you." She looked over her shoulder to make sure no one was eavesdropping. "*In person.*" Gina's eyes were like saucers. "And he looked thunderous."

"Calm down, Gina. Probably just an issue with ZurichZeit. They've been a bit high maintenance lately. But it's nothing we can't fix with a little hand-holding." Gina was a fantastic assistant. Highly organized and detail oriented. But she also had a penchant for melodrama. Apparently, she'd been a theater major in college. "Do me a favor?" she asked, keeping her pace unhurried. "Book me on an afternoon flight to LaGuardia? And use my miles to upgrade me to first class?" There was a champagne glass and a linen napkin waiting for her with her name on it. Maybe she'd chat up a nice businessman. Anything to get her mind off the buff cowboy who held her heart.

Strolling into her office, she grabbed her phone. Her eyes widened at the onslaught of notifications. Gina hadn't been kidding. Her heart kicked up a notch as worry threaded through her. Had something catastrophic happened to her family? Had a bomb gone off somewhere? She thumbed through to the top of the notifications. The first had been from Alex Jordan, not thirty seconds after she'd left for the rooftop.

A: Call me. We need to talk asap

Then three missed calls, all from Alex.
Then 2 missed calls from Travis, and a text.

T: Where in the hell are you? Call me.

Her heart started racing. She went through where everyone was supposed to be this morning. Maddie would be teaching at K-State until two. Her brothers would all be out on the ranch. Hope was driving back from Oklahoma… Her stomach sank. Oh God, had there been an accident? Or worse, a tornado? That would explain why Mr. Prince had come looking for her.

Her heart smashed into her throat when her extension rang. She steadied her shaking hand as she answered. "This is Emma."

"Prince. I need you in my office immediately."

"Yes, sir. I'll be right there."

The air left Emma's lungs, and she struggled to grab air. Her palms started to sweat. Grabbing her phone, she trotted down the hall to the Owner's office. Her phone buzzed three times in the thirty seconds it took to reach his door.

"It's open," he called as she raised her hand to knock. He was standing at the window, hands in his pockets as she entered. "Shut the door."

The door swung shut with an ominous click. "Is everything okay?"

The older man who had been her mentor since her sophomore year in college looked at her, brown eyes hard as steel.

"I don't know how to have this conversation, Emma."

"Oh God." She interrupted him for the first time in her life. "Please tell me my family is okay?"

His mouth thinned. "They're fine, but they won't be by the end of the day."

"I don't understand."

He inhaled, nostrils flaring. "I have never, in my forty-two years of running a company had an hour like the last one."

"What's going on?"

"Shall I start with the failure to comply with a non-disclosure resulting in a lawsuit? Or the indecent exposure of one of my employees caught *in flagrante* with a client?"

"Did something happen with ZurichZeit?" She mentally rescheduled her trip to New York, deciding to ask Gina to find her an overnight to Zurich. Maybe she needed to pay them another visit.

The tension crackled off her boss. "If only. Are you sure there isn't anything you want to… disclose to me?"

She shook her head. "I'm so sorry. I have no idea what you're talking about."

He pointed to an envelope on the table by the window. "Let's see if this jogs your memory."

She pulled the papers out of the envelope, quickly scanning. Heat raced up her spine as she read the civil suit from Kaycee accusing her and Royal Fountain of breaching a non-disclosure.

Was this what Travis had been calling about? "I don't understand. There are only four others who know about Kaycee. We all signed."

"This alone would be grounds for dismissal."

"I understand, but I didn't *do* anything, sir. I've followed protocol to the letter."

"Have you? I also received a call less than an hour ago from a reporter at *The Pitch* asking me to comment on a story they are running this afternoon. Something involving a sex tape between an employee and Alex Jordan of the Kansas City Kings?"

"*What?*" The blood rushed to her toes, leaving her body hot then cold.

"No need to act surprised, Emma. There's no doubt it's you." He sounded resigned. Disgusted.

This couldn't be happening. She and Alex had secretly dated for about six months, and during that time, they'd... played around. But she'd deleted every video in her possession. And there was no way Alex would let them be seen, if he even still had them. She opened her mouth but no sound came out.

Mr. Prince's cheeks flushed. "Don't worry, I stopped it as soon as I recognized you." He shut his eyes, grimacing. "You've been with us for eight years, Emma. Eight years."

"Sir, I don't know–"

He raised his hand. "Stop. You've shown so much promise over the years, and I had been looking forward to promoting you this summer."

Panic hollowed her stomach. This couldn't be happening. That tone of voice. The look on his face. "I can explain. Please let me explain."

"Royal Fountain has always prided itself on its standards of excellence and discretion. Our reputation is impeccable. Unassailable. I know that you know we have a strict no fraternization policy with our clients, as well as confidentiality clauses. We discussed this the first day of your internship eight years ago. You've seen colleagues let go for lesser offenses."

She braced herself for the guillotine.

Mr. Prince shook his head. "I'm so sorry. But I need to request your resignation. Effective immediately."

She cried out as the shock of it sank in. "Mr. Prince. I don't know how this could have happened. I really don't."

He smiled wryly. "Usually, it starts with inappropriate sexual relations."

She'd have laughed out loud if she wasn't so horrified. Was this why Alex had called her? To warn her? Anger surged through her. He'd promised to destroy their playful evidence. And why now after they'd been broken up for two years? None of this made sense.

She locked her knees as a wave of nausea rocked her. Her clients... what would this do to her fundraising efforts for the ranch? She could lose all of them. And she wouldn't be allowed to contact them after she left the office. This could ruin everything. Hell, who was she kidding? It *had* ruined everything. "Mr. Prince? Please, the donors who've offered to sponsor the fundraiser at Resolution Ranch. May I please be allowed to contact them?"

His eyes softened, then filled with regret. "I'm sorry. We have those rules in place for a reason."

She must be having a heart attack. She couldn't feel her fingers and her lips started to tingle. Was she having a hallucination? A waking nightmare? Maybe someone had slipped drugs in her coffee. But if that was the case, she shouldn't be able to hear the tick-tocking of the wall clock behind his desk. Filling the silence, demanding that she say something. She stifled a sob, wanting nothing more than for the earth to swallow her whole. "I understand. I'm sure someone will be contacting them to explain the situation?"

He nodded. "And we'll give them the opportunity to stay on, provided you are not their point of contact."

"I understand. I can arrange for Ster-, the ranch foreman to take over with anyone who wants to stay on." She took a deep breath. "Is there anything else, sir?"

He faced the window again, dismissing her. "I think that's quite enough."

"Mr. Prince?"

He turned his head.

"I'm so very sorry about this."

"I am, too. Please leave your company technology on your desk. Someone will show you out."

Leaving his office in a fog, she blindly retraced her steps to her office. Her phone buzzed again. She clung to it like a lifeline, refusing to check it until she was seated at her desk for the last time. She waved off Gina and made a beeline for her chair, collapsing into it, shaking like a leaf.

"You're booked on the three-ten to New York," Gina said quietly, placing a steaming cup of coffee on the desk in front of her.

"Good, I'll need it," she answered dryly before turning over her phone.

On her screen was a text from Travis and a link.

T: What the *fuck* is this?!?!?

She clicked the link, then choked on her coffee, nearly spitting it out. A headline read *Kaycee Starr discovered hiding in Kansas.* The video she'd taken of Kaycee singing in the barn, took up most of the page, and below, a short paragraph offered all the details.

Country music darling, Kaycee Starr, has been hiding out in Prairie, Kansas, apparently working on a new album. Her agent could not be reached with details.

She put her head on the desk, focusing on the cool wood beneath her forehead. The video had gone viral, with thousands of comments and hundreds of thousands of views. She dialed Travis as the pieces started to fall into place.

"You better have a damned good explanation for this," he growled, not bothering with niceties. "Paparazzi are crawling all over town like cockroaches."

"Travis, I swear, I'm as surprised as you are. And I don't understand why this had to escalate to a lawsuit."

"Do you understand what this is going to cost her? And us?"

"I do. Sterling is the only person who saw the video, and then he insisted we come see you. Which we did."

"Well the cat's out of the bag now, and Kate and Cash have gone underground. And I think that pretty much ruins our chances for a concert in three weeks."

"*No.* I can fix this. I won't let you down."

"You've already let me down. How could you be so careless with that video?"

"I wasn't. I had my phone–" Shit. Her phone. Her body clenched. "My phone. Travis. Whoever stole my phone must have hacked it." Her brain went numb. What else had they discovered? But those videos had been deleted years ago.

Gina waved at her from the doorway, motioning that someone was coming. Great. Could her world be more fucked up?

"This is a disaster, Emma. A total fucking disaster."

No shit, Sherlock, she wanted to snap.

A security guard hovered in the doorway. Of course. Because now she needed to be publicly escorted out of the building. "Travis, can I call you back? I swear I'll do whatever I can to make this right. And I hate to do this, but I have to run."

She handed the security guard her laptop and her company phone as her personal phone rang again. "Alex. I think I know what happened."

"Emma, what in the hell is going on? You told me you deleted that stuff."

"I *did,*" she cried out. "I–" Her stomach pitched as she marched down the hall to the elevator, security guard trailing behind with a small box of her personal items. "I think my devices got hacked."

"*What?* Didn't you wipe your drive? You're always supposed to wipe your drive." She didn't even know how to do that. That's why every company had a tech department. The horror of everything began to sink in as the elevator opened. "Can I call you back?" she said with a hysterical giggle. "I'm in the process of getting sacked." She followed the security guard into the elevator and let the call drop.

Forty-five silent seconds later, she stood on the sidewalk on Main holding a small cardboard box, spring sun blazing brightly, breeze dancing down the street, her life in tatters at her feet.

CHAPTER 28

T HE RANCH WAS in chaos. Weston had sent a patrol car to block the drive. No one knew where Cash and Kate were, and that left Sterling and Travis to run double duty on the chores. Elaine repeatedly offered her help, but Travis insisted she stay inside with her feet up.

"I'm not a china doll," she exclaimed with exasperation.

"But you *are* seven and a half months pregnant, and I don't want to risk you getting injured by a spooked horse."

"Then let Dax come with you. He's old enough to rake the hay."

"Please, Dad? Can I help, please?"

Travis looked from his stepson to his wife, and Sterling had to smile. The man was crazy about them. He nodded curtly, only to be assaulted at the legs by Dax wrapping him in a bear hug.

Something in Travis's expression punched him in the gut. Jealousy snaked through him. Travis had it all. The woman, the kids, the life. He made it look so damned easy. And the smile on his face said it all. The man was as happy as a pig in mud. Even with funding for the ranch in jeopardy, paparazzi trespassing, and two employees on the run.

Travis kissed Elaine tenderly and held out his hand to Dax. "You ready to help young man?"

"Does that mean I'm a real cowboy?"

"Indeed." The three of them made their way to the barn, Dax skipping ahead. "Dax, your job is to muck the stalls. Remember, never enter a stall with a horse. Understood?"

"You bet, Dad." Dax skipped down the aisle to the far end of the barn where the wheelbarrows and shovels stood next to the pile of fresh hay.

"How do you do it?" Sterling asked once Dax was out of earshot. "Stay so calm?"

Travis made a face. "Believe me, I'm anything but calm."

"I don't follow."

"All we can do is control our own reactions. I have no control over Cash sweeping Kate off to some undisclosed location to keep her away from the media and crazed fans. I have no control over Emma's devices getting hacked. I might get gruff, but I'm not going to lose my shit anymore. All I can do is work to stay calm, and choose how I'm going to respond. And I'm sure as hell not going to do anything that scares Dax, or upsets Elaine."

"Do you ever worry you're going to lose it again?"

Travis regarded him steadily. "Sure. But you learn to take each day at a time. Sometimes each moment at a time. The key is to keep moving through it."

The words were out before Sterling could pull them back. "I'm afraid I'm going to lose my shit. Go off half-cocked. Or worse." His heart pounded at the admission. He looked up to the older man. Didn't want Travis thinking he couldn't handle being here. But Sterling couldn't get a read on him. No one could keep a poker face like Travis.

"That have anything to do with the yelling the other night?" Travis cocked a brow, face unmoving.

Shame slithered down Sterling's neck. Fuck. Who else had heard? Sterling let out a shaky breath. "I'm having a rough time with Johnny's death."

Travis nodded his understanding. "It's never easy losing someone you love. Especially when you think you could have prevented their deaths."

Something eased inside him. "You too?"

Travis lifted a shoulder. "All I can tell you is the hurt dims in time. But the wound is never completely healed."

"I–" Sterling raked a hand through his hair. "I can't get over this idea that I'm gonna end up like Johnny."

"You ever talked to anyone about that?"

Sterling shook his head.

"No shame in talking to someone."

The thought of exposing his vulnerable underbelly to a perfect stranger didn't sit well with him.

As if sensing his uncertainty, Travis pressed his point. "Doesn't make you weak. Or less of a man. In fact, some would say it makes you more of one, and a better leader, knowing when to ask for help." Travis ducked into the feed room and began to measure out feed for the horses. "You've heard me say it before, but it bears repeating. You gonna let Johnny's story *be* your story? Or just be a part of your story?"

Sterling squirmed inside as he took the feed and marched it down to the farthest stall.

Travis followed, hitting the next stall. "I'm gonna offer my unsolicited opinion," he said as he dumped the grains in the feedbag and returned to the grain bins for the next batch. He stopped his measuring and hit him with a weighty gaze. "From what I've seen, it sounds like Johnny's story has taken over."

The secret part of him, the one that ate at him at night for pushing Emma away, the one that called him out for being an idiot, behaving like an ass… That secret part kicked him in the nuts. He was living some weird stunted version of Johnny's life.

"Sorry to interrupt, but I got a bone to pick with you gents," Brodie Sinclaire drawled from the barn entrance.

Sterling froze. Brodie's tall grass threat returned to him in a rush. The last thing he wanted was an altercation with Brodie, even though the secret part of him shouted he deserved a good pounding.

As usual, Travis seemed unfazed. "Talk to me, Brodie."

"Seems my little sister is in a peck of trouble." His gaze swept between the two of them. "And the ranch seems to be at the center of the shit show."

Travis handed Brodie a feed bucket and motioned for him to follow. "That so? She mention anything to you about a violation of a non-disclosure agreement and a viral video? Or the fact I've got paparazzi crawling over my property like the plague and now I'm two employees short with three more houses to build before May 1st?"

"My wife tells me Em's being sued by Kaycee Star and was canned this morning."

The news hit Sterling with the force of an earthquake. "She lost her job?"

Brodie turned the full force of his ire on him. "Seems like she was on the receiving end of a double whammy this morning." His eyes narrowed. "Some assfuck put a video of my sister and Alex Jordan showing a little too much skin, if you get my drift, on the internet today, and that shit's gone viral."

"I'll kill 'em," Sterling muttered under his breath. Sterling fisted a hand. So help him, he'd track Alex down and pound him into the pavement. Major league baseball star be damned. A sex video? Bile reached up into his throat. The thought of

Emma doing anything they'd enjoyed together with another man made his skin burn as if he'd been attacked by a nest of fire ants. But what kind of low-life made that shit public? That was the bigger offense.

"Get in line," Brodie snarled.

"Now hold on." Travis took Brodie's bucket and poured it into Bingo's feed bag. "There's a video of Emma and Alex too?"

"What do you mean, *too*?" Brodie was clearly struggling to hold onto his temper. As was Sterling.

Travis sighed heavily. "Did Jamey tell you that Emma's devices were stolen at the baseball game and she was hacked?"

"She was a touch upset. I didn't get much out of her beyond the cursing."

Travis smiled wryly. "Emma has footage of Kaycee here at the ranch. The material is, *was*, confidential. Until this morning, when it got posted and went viral. Hence the lawsuit, and the sacking.

"Have you talked to Emma?" Sterling asked. Emma must be beside herself. She'd put so much effort into her fundraising efforts for the ranch.

"She won't talk to anyone. Jamey's brother's a lawyer, so he's offered to help, but these kinds of lawsuits aren't his specialty."

Sterling's mind was whirling. He turned to Travis. "Jason Case will know who to talk to. We have to help Emma."

Travis gave him a hard stare. "Do we?"

"Of course we do. We can't let her swing in the wind after all she's done for the ranch." And while she was distracted because he'd behaved like an ass. "And we have to convince Kate to call off the dogs. We have to find her."

Brodie crossed his arms, still glowering. "That would be a

step in the right direction."

For a moment, no one spoke. Sterling got the distinct feeling Travis was sizing him up. Weighing him in the balance and perhaps, finding him wanting. Right then, he vowed to be better. To do better. To ask Travis who he could talk to, and to start living his own story, not Johnny's.

Travis drew in a deep breath and raised his eyes skyward. "I don't know where they are, but I know how Cash thinks and I have a hunch I know where to look." He patted his chest pocket. "Anyone have pen and paper?"

"I've got my phone." Sterling pulled his phone from his jean jacket pocket, and handed it over.

Travis typed for a minute and handed it back. Sterling blinked. "You're kidding?"

"It's worth a shot. I think there's a four p.m. flight from Manhattan."

"I'll never make it."

"Looks like you'll be driving then."

Ten long agonizing hours later, Sterling entered *Navy One*, one of two high-rise apartments overlooking Navy Pier. Strung out on adrenaline and truck stop coffee, he was ready to collapse, but not until he's spoken with Cash and Kate. If they were even here. Deep in his gut, he knew they were. It was clever, really. Hiding a country star in a swanky high-rise apartment in the city like Chicago.

The night guard stopped him.

"I'm here to see Cash Aiken."

The night guard scowled suspiciously. "At ten minutes to three in the morning?"

The last of Sterling's patience frayed. "I have been driving for the last ten hours. It's extremely important that I speak to Cash."

The guard clicked his tongue. "I will need you to wait while I verify that," he said firmly. No wonder Travis suspected Cash might be here. The security guard was a shark.

"Tell him Sterling is here and I've driven all night."

A few minutes later, the guard returned, shaking his head. "Count yourself lucky. The elevator is around the corner."

The elevator ride was the longest of his life, and the doors opened to a hall eerily silent. The carpet absorbed his footfalls, but Cash must have been listening for the elevator bell, because as he was about to knock, the door whipped open, and Cash stood there, glaring. "I should break every bone in your body."

"I know, I know. Can I please come in?"

Cash stepped aside and Sterling stepped into a luxurious condo with floor to ceiling windows overlooking Navy Pier and the black beyond of Lake Michigan.

Sterling whistled low. "Nice digs. This place yours?"

Cash nodded curtly as he stalked to the window. "Bought it when I got out. But it's been used as a safe house before. Hard for people to spy on you from the water." He bent and tossed him a blanket. "You're sleeping on the couch. We'll talk in the morning." Cash spun and stalked back to the bedroom without so much as a sound. Sterling kicked off his boots and lay down on the couch, pulling the rough wool blanket up to his shoulders. Exhaustion settled in his bones and his eyelids grew heavy. The blessed relief of sleep hovered just out of reach.

Tonight, maybe, he'd sleep with a lighter heart. The hours in the truck had given him more than enough time to examine every aspect of his life under a microscope. Travis was right. Jason and Macey were right. He needed to live Sterling's life, not Johnny's death. He honored Johnny's memory not by existing the way Johnny had at the end, but by living the way Johnny had when they'd been younger. "I'll make this right, Em. I swear," he mumbled as sleep claimed him.

CHAPTER 29

THE GENTLE SOUNDS of guitar strings coupled with brilliant sunlight, woke Sterling a few hours later. Kate sat on a low chair across from the couch, humming and scratching a pencil across paper. She glanced across when he stirred, catching his eye. The lines on her face gave away her weariness. Her exhaustion. She gave him a small smile. "Morning. Coffee?"

He raised a hand. "Don't trouble yourself. I'll grab some."

"Cash is in the kitchen."

Shaking the cobwebs from his head, he stood, following his nose to the coffee pot. Cash handed him a steaming mug. "So I take it this isn't a social call?"

"Nope."

Cash pushed off the counter and stalked out of the kitchen. "Let's get this over with then."

Sterling followed him and settled himself back on the couch, taking in the view. No wonder Cash had bought the place. There was a serenity in the view that calmed the rough places in his soul.

Cash stood in the corner, staring out the window, back ramrod straight. Tension radiated off him in waves. Sterling shifted his attention back to Kate who looked equally ill at ease. But he hadn't driven all night long for awkward silences. He'd fix this for Emma, or die trying. "Emma didn't post your video. She'd never do that. Not in a million years. The ranch means too much to her. Her devices got stolen the day of the baseball game. Whoever nabbed them hacked them."

Cash spun, giving Sterling a hard look as he whipped out his phone. "Those sons of bitches picked the wrong people to fuck with," he growled. Cash disappeared into the kitchen and returned a minute later. "I've got people working on reverse tracing the IP addresses from the video.

Sterling stared at him. "You can do that?"

Cash's eyes grew flinty. "And a whole lot more."

An idea struck him. "Do you know about the other videos?"

"What other videos?" Cash grumbled, shoulders bunching.

"Some douchenozzle who I would dearly love to strangle, posted videos of Emma and Alex Jordan in... er... compromising positions."

Kate gasped, covering her mouth. "Have you seen them?"

"Never," Sterling spat. "I don't ever want to see them. But I want to nail the motherfucker who did this."

Cash gave him a cold smile. "I have people who may be able to help." He disappeared down the hall.

Sterling cleared his throat. "I have an idea about how to fix everything and I'm hoping you'll hear me out?"

Kate regarded him steadily through tired eyes, then nodded. His gut clenched. She looked like she'd given up, and he hated seeing that. "First. I have a friend with a friend—"

Cash made a scoffing noise as he returned, this time with the coffee pot. "Did Kate tell you that her agent is suing her for breach of contract *even though she fired him last fall?*"

Sterling raised his cup, accepting a refill. The prevalence of assholes in the world never ceased to amaze him. "I'm not shitting you, Kate. On my honor. I have a friend who is connected to a shark of a lawyer in Hollywood. Represents movie stars in disputes. If your agent is wrongly suing you–"

"He is."

"If you feel your agent is wrongly suing you, she will take your case pro bono as a favor to my friend."

Kaycee made a doubtful noise. "Forgive my suspicion."

"I understand. You don't know who to trust. If you like, you can talk to my friend Jason first. He'll be returning to the ranch as part of the first program just before the concert, and I can assure you, he's solid."

She still looked dubious, but nodded her head.

"What else," Cash growled.

"In return, I would ask that you drop your suit against Emma. Royal Fountain sacked her because of the Alex Jordan videos."

Kate chewed on her lip.

"Look." Sterling held up his phone. "Your video went viral. It's had over four million views since it was posted yesterday. And read the comments. People love it. They want more." He took a deep breath. "I know Emma asked you to sing at the concert. Is there any chance you'd reconsider?"

Worry pulled at her face.

Sterling held up his hands. "Even just a few songs? As a gift to the donors supporting the ranch. Think of it as a no-pressure opportunity for you to get your feet back under you." He waved the phone. "You already have proof people will love it."

"But the security…" her voice trailed off uncertainly as she cast a fear-filled look at Cash.

"I won't let you out of my sight for a second," he growled.

"I can work with Travis and Weston to manage the paparazzi." Winning this little victory suddenly took on much more weight. "Whatever it takes. I know it would mean a lot to the ranch if you would consider joining the concert. And to Emma too," he added after a pause. "And I'm sure if you give her the chance, Emma would help you with the media. Make a press release, or anything else you want." He wasn't even sure Emma would speak to him ever again. But he was convinced if Kate asked for help, she'd give it. She'd never turn her back on anyone.

Sterling's heart twisted. He'd turned his back on her. Never again. What had Travis said about moment by moment? If he could manage to let his love for Emma be the guiding force of *this* moment, that would be a step forward. If he could salvage this for her, afford her a tiny victory, maybe it would be a tiny victory for him too. And maybe someday she'd come to forgive him, even if she never spoke to him again.

Kate looked up at Cash, and they exchanged a meaningful glance.

Sterling shifted uncomfortably. Was his presence here an intrusion? Kate looked between the two of them, and rolled back her shoulders, suddenly looking determined. "Can you get me a microphone and a laptop?"

For the first time in a long time, hope flickered in his chest. "Anything."

"I'll do it."

CHAPTER 30

I N THE END, the hacking cost the ranch a hundred grand. Although Brodie assured her that Cash and Weston were using all their sources to track the culprit, three weeks had passed and still no leads.

But surprisingly, the lawsuit against her and Royal Fountain had been dropped. And she hadn't even had to talk to Jamey's brother the lawyer. Then to her absolute shock, Kate had called her and promised to perform at the concert, telling her she'd go public with her appearance and use it to launch an EP with four new songs, giving all the proceeds to the ranch. Proceeds from those sales alone might recoup the lost funding from the donors she'd lost.

Emma sat listlessly scrolling job postings on LinkedIn. The lodge was quiet at the moment, but with guests arriving in a few hours for the poker tournament and concert the following day, Brodie and Jamey had asked her to move back to her room at the Big House. It wasn't that she didn't love the Big House. She adored Blake and Maddie and little Henry. Even her half-brother Simon, who lived at the ranch nearly full-time now. They were great. But they functioned like a family. She swallowed down the painful lump that lodged itself deep in her throat.

For a brief moment, she'd allowed herself to dream. To believe that a family like theirs might be in her future. But the fantasy had dissipated with a *poof.* She clicked on a job posting in New York City. She was qualified, and the salary was good. She had infinite connections in NYC, most of them from her time at Barnard, and removed from her celebrity as Kansas City's newest porn star.

Alex had been a champ, hiring an assistant specifically to troll the internet for new video postings and then immediately sending out take-down notices. But the effort was more like whack-a-mole. Eventually the chatter would die down. But until then, she had no choice but to avoid all of the spring fundraisers and galas she'd attended in the past.

She closed the tab with a sigh and snapped the laptop shut. Who was she kidding? She loved visiting her friends in New York, loved visiting, but she didn't want to live there. It was too far away from her family. She'd miss Henry's first time on a pony by himself. Or when Blake started him in pee-wee soccer. Or sheep wrangling at the county fair.

Jamey breezed in from the kitchen, a determined expression on her face, holding a bottle of liquor. Behind her followed Lydia Grace and Emmaline carrying glasses, Luci Cruz carrying a plate of her famous tamales, and her sister-in-law Hope. Jamey set the bottle down in front of her with a *thunk.* "Time for you to stop mooning around the lodge like a lovesick puppy."

Emma's spine snapped straight. "I'm *not* a lovesick puppy."

Jamey's answering look said otherwise. "So you'll admit to mooning then?"

Emma answered with a ghost of a smile. "Maybe a little."

Jamey unscrewed the cap and began pouring. "Twelve-year Redbreast. Magic of the Leprechauns. Also known as the crisis bottle." She passed the glasses of amber liquid to each of the women.

"We might not be able to help Sterling pull his head out of his ass, but I bet the men will take care of that."

"But how do you? I don't understand."

Lydia scoffed. "*Puhleeze*, Emma. Anyone who saw the two of you even look at each other could tell something was up."

"But we're here today to talk about *you*. About your future. With or without Cowboy McDouchebag."

"He's *not* a douchebag," Emma snapped.

"No?" Jamey's eyes grew fierce. "Well, he's going to have to work hard to get back into my good graces."

"Mine too," Hope added.

Emma raised a hand. "Whoa, whoa guys. Sterling has baggage, and until he works through that, he's not good for anyone, least of all himself. I'm a big girl. I jumped in where maybe I shouldn't have. But don't be mean to him when you see him tomorrow. Please? Don't make this any harder than it already is."

Emmaline cleared her throat. "Can we get back to the more important discussion? How to help Em?"

"Right," Jamey said, lifting her glass. "Cheers to you Em. You've helped all of us improve our businesses this spring."

Emmaline nodded vigorously. "It never even occurred to me that people would want to come to me for my dress designs." She looked at the other women. "Outside of Prairie, I mean. I have a waiting list for wedding dresses for this summer."

Emma's face flushed. "Really? That's wonderful news."

"That wouldn't have happened without you, Emma. So, thanks."

"Have you ever thought about starting your own agency?" asked Hope. "I mean, look at all of us. We're all women, and all small business owners. We could use someone like you in our corner. Especially with your connections outside of Prairie."

Lydia piped up. "I think we could all help each other. Emma and I both have connections in New York."

"As do I, and in Paris and Chicago," added Jamey. "If you helped us with marketing and publicity, together our connections could help so many others. I mean, have you tasted a tamale as good as this?" She gestured to the plate Luci had brought in.

Something sparked to life deep inside Emma. "When I first became an Athena Scholar, I knew I wanted to run my own business someday. I just didn't know what. I don't have the talent you women do. I'm not an artist."

Lydia made a disbelieving noise in the back of her throat. "You don't think marketing is an art? I beg to differ. I might make a sexy pair of boots, but what good is that if the world doesn't know about them? Or get excited about them?"

The other women nodded their agreement.

"Main Street is reopening tomorrow," Luci said. "And it's more important than ever that those businesses thrive. You could help all of us."

"But I can't work at the kitchen table. I'd need an office."

Jamey smirked. "Too bad you don't have three older brothers to wrap around your finger and build you what you need on the property."

"There are a couple of vacant bunkhouses on my family's property," Hope suggested. "I could talk to Dad and Gunn, I'm sure they'd let you use one while you get up and running."

"I'm probably going to have to sell my condo now that I'm unemployed. But I could use the equity as seed money." A thrill of excitement set her blood pumping. She could see herself doing this. "Maybe even rent an office on Main."

Emmaline clapped her hands. "Ooh. What about the vacant space next to my dress shop? I don't know that anything's gone in there yet. And there's an apartment above it."

"Mom will know who owns that building," Lydia said.

"Who has a napkin?" Emma asked, an idea popping into her head. Luci pushed a notebook and pen across to her with a smile. "I was hoping I'd hear you say that."

Emma tapped the pen, then opened to a blank page and began to sketch. When she was finished, she turned the paper around.

Em+Power

"Em-Power Creative. Media solutions for the modern age."

Lydia clapped her hands. "*Love. It.*"

"I'll toast to that." Jamey grinned, raising her glass.

"For now, I'll focus my energy on women-owned companies."

"You'll have more business than you can handle," crowed Luci. "I just know it."

Confidence surged through Emma as she looked around the table. She did too.

CHAPTER 31

THE WOMEN MUST have made some kind of a pact to never leave Emma alone. They'd circled her like mama elephants with a baby, flapping their ears at anyone who ventured too close. How in the hell was he supposed to explain himself in front of them? They'd judged him, and he'd come up short.

Jason clapped him on the shoulder. "Are you going to talk to her or just stare at her all day?"

"They're like fruit flies. I can't get within ten feet of her before one of them swoops in and starts talking to her, or drags her off," he growled.

Jason chuckled. "Time to man up. You need to show your girl how much she means to you.

"She's not my girl," he mumbled.

"But you want her to be?"

Sterling nodded. "More than anything."

"Then don't sit on your ass, go get her."

Sterling's feet were moving before Jason had finished talking. Jason's laughter followed him as he crossed Main Street to where she stood outside a vacant storefront next door to Emmaline's newly re-opened dress shop. He loved seeing Main Street shiny and new. Thanks to Emma, the businesses had decided to wait until today and reopen all at once. The result would be an all-day party that ended with the poker tournament and concert at Resolution Ranch.

"Emma," he called and five pairs of eyes turned to him. Did they have to stand so close together? "You have a sec? I'd love to talk to you."

His hands turned sweaty as one of the women gave her a little push forward.

"Hi Sterling," Luci Cruz said brightly. "What do you think about this storefront? She motioned to the storefront. "We're trying to convince Emma it's the perfect place for her new business."

New business? Was she moving back to Prairie? Hope flamed to life in his chest. If she moved home to Prairie, pursuing her, making things up to her, would be so much easier. Although he'd willingly drive to Kansas City every day if that's what it took.

"I think it looks great," he said, meaning it. He looked her right in the eye. Those beautiful big blue eyes tinged with sadness. His gut twisted painfully. He owned some of that pain. He'd do what it took to erase it. "I think you'll be great."

"You needed something?" She looked unsure.

"We'll be right across the street if you need us," Luci said loudly enough for him to hear. He understood her meaning. *We'll be right here if he's an asshole.* But he wouldn't be an asshole this time. The framed artwork she'd given him popped into his head. *Never never never give up.* No way he was giving up. Not when he finally knew what he wanted. Who he wanted.

The women melted away, leaving the two of them standing alone. Sterling's heart beat erratically, and his lungs emptied. He couldn't catch his breath. He reached for her hand. "Can we go sit someplace?" His voice didn't sound like his own. But he'd be damned if he was going to stand here in the middle of Main Street and bare his soul while the entire town looked on.

She nodded. More importantly, she didn't remove her hand. He led her down the street and around the corner. Neither of them spoke, but an electric current fused their hands together, speaking in a way words could not. Behind the Lutheran church, a little pocket park had survived the previous year's tornado. As he entered the secluded space, the scent of peonies filled the air. He pulled her to the stone bench that sat tucked under a maple sapling.

He drew her hand to his lap, tracing her fingers with his own. "Emma, I know I'm going to fuck this up, so please be patient. Please hear me out."

She turned the full force of her gaze to him. It gutted him, seeing her like this, knowing he was the cause. In trying to protect her, he'd brought about the very thing he'd tried to avoid. He cupped her face. "You are so incredibly perfect. Kind and strong and fearless. You do everything with this level of excellence that always pushes me to be better. Even when you're not there. My life is so incredibly empty without you in it. And I'm ashamed at how I fucked everything up."

Her eyes shimmered in the dappled light.

He rushed on. "I was so scared I'd turn into Johnny. So scared I'd make you as sad as Macey, that I was an idiot. And I hurt you anyway. And I'm so, so sorry. I was a coward, and Johnny would have kicked my ass for pushing you away."

A tear slid down her cheek, wetting his thumb.

"The Johnny I knew before he got depressed wasn't scared of anything. He lived big. And he went after anything he wanted. And I think I told you how he pursued Macey with the same single-mindedness that he pursued his missions.

With everything he had. And on the long drive to Chicago I had a lot of time to think."

Her eyes jumped wide open. "Wait. When did you go to Chicago?"

He shook his head. "Long story. And I'll tell you all of it another time. What's important is that I had a long time to think." He grabbed both her hands and clasped them to his chest. "Love is worse than Ranger school."

Emma snorted.

"I don't mean that in a bad way. I mean it in an *Oh Shit* way. The things they have you do – jumping out of planes, live ammo training, survival training in brutal conditions, it scares the shit out of you, but you do it anyway because you want it so bad. You endure the pain for the gratification."

"So why is love worse?"

"Because there are no guarantees."

Emma's brows knitted together. "But there aren't in Ranger School either, are there?"

"It's different. Sure, there are training accidents, but death is rare. The point is you do things that scare the shit out of you, endure the impossible, because you know in the end, you'll be welcomed into an elite group comprising the best of the best. And you leave it all on the field in the hopes you'll pass."

"And love isn't like that," Emma filled in. "You leave it all on the field and you may come up empty and alone."

Sterling nodded. "Yeah. That."

"So when there's a mark to hit, it's easy to throw everything you have into hitting the mark."

"Exactly. When I went through Ranger school, I knew I had no choice but to keep going. Because I couldn't live with myself if I'd let fear decide. But I let fear make the calls between us. And if you'll let me try again, I'll leave it all on the field for you."

She regarded him uncertainly.

This was it. This was his Hail Mary. He cupped her face between his hands. "I wasn't there for you when the shit hit the fan, and I should've been. If I hadn't been such a dick, maybe your stuff wouldn't have gotten stolen."

She let out a tiny laugh but it sounded more like a sob, and she covered one of his hands with her own, pressing it against her cheek. "I left my car unlocked. I should have known better. Even in Prairie."

"I swear, I will skin the culprits alive bit by bit when we find them," he ground out.

"I was terrified you'd be so mad about the video you'd never talk to me again."

"Oh, I'm jealous as fuck." He kissed her forehead. Then the tip of her nose. Then left the barest of kisses on her lips. "I want to be your man. Your only. But I didn't behave in a way that deserves that honor. However – I will happily spend the rest of my days showing you how much you mean to me. I only want you, Emma." He almost missed her smile it was so fleeting. "I said awful things I can't unsay. But hopefully, new words will erase the old ones in time?"

Her eyes clouded and she laid her palm over his heart. "I believe in you, Sterling. Believe you can be the man you want to be. That you can help prevent other veterans from choosing the same fate as Johnny. And I'm so, so proud of you." She drew in a shaky breath and met his eyes. "But I'm scared. More than anything I want to believe that you're not going to break me. That you're going to give us a chance with everything you've got. That you'll fight for us."

"I will, babe. I promise. I can't promise I'll do it perfectly, or that I won't fuck up. But you have my word as an officer and a gentleman that I will do whatever it takes to make you believe in *us*. To show you how much I love you, and how much you mean to me."

She gave him a crooked smile and his face burned.

Fuck. He hadn't meant for that to slip out so soon. But he was going to fucking own it. "You heard right, babe. I love you. Heck, maybe I've loved you since you sassed me playing baseball in the seventh grade, and I was too dumb or arrogant to figure it out."

Two more tears slid over her cheeks and she giggled. "I'd like to meet your parents. Get to know the Sterling no one knows."

"From here on out, I'm an open book. I'll bring you to breakfast tomorrow. You'll love my mom."

"Sterling?"

He pressed his forehead against hers, heart pounding the way it did the first time he jumped out of a plane.

"I love you, too."

CHAPTER 32

Six weeks later...

E MMA CHECKED HER phone while she paced in front of
the plate glass window now etched with the logo
Em+Power Creative. Her heart pounded. In the grand scheme
of things today wasn't that big of a deal. And yet... her heart
pounded like it was her first kiss.

Sterling wrapped his arms around her from behind, plant-
ing little kisses on her neck. "Ready for your big day? The
window looks great."

"I'm nervous. It's one thing to work from my living room
upstairs, it's another to commit to an office."

"You're ready for it. You've worked hard." He turned her
around, wrapping his hands around her shoulders. "You're
going to be a wild success, babe. Look at all the clients you
already have and you haven't technically opened yet. You'll be
hiring an assistant in no time."

She pulled him in for a hug, and lifted her face for a kiss.
"It's corny to say this, but I need to thank you."

"How so?"

"If all that bad business hadn't happened, I never would
have considered opening my own agency."

His face clouded. "I hate that my being a jerk caused you
pain. But I'm glad it worked out in the end. All of it."

"Me, too." She grinned up at him. Whatever the future

brought them, they would face it together.

Emmaline pushed open the door next to hers. "Ready?" She smiled brightly. Lydia trailed right behind her, holding a box with a blue ribbon.

Her brothers, all of them – Blake, Brodie, Ben and even her half-brother Simon, pulled up in front of the building, and hopped out of Brodie's truck one by one.

She checked her phone again. Three minutes to nine.

Dottie and Jamey bustled down the street holding trays of coffee. Millie rounded the corner carrying a bouquet of flowers.

Brodie checked his phone. "Where is everyone? We have two minutes."

"Oh calm down. It's not the end of the world if it's nine-o-three," Emma chided.

Luci skipped up holding two grocery bags. Before the aroma registered, Emma knew she'd brought tamales, and she salivated at the prospect of the upcoming feast.

Finally, two trucks emblazoned with the Resolution Ranch logo pulled to a stop across the street. Cash, Kate, and Jason made their way across the street while Travis helped a very pregnant Elaine.

Dottie looked around. "I think we're all here, sweetie pie. You ready?"

Her sisters-in-law Maddie and Hope, pushing Henry in a stroller, hurried up. "I'm so sorry we're late," said Hope breathlessly. "We didn't miss it, did we?"

"You're right on time." Emma looked around the little group assembled and her eyes prickled. Her family, her friends, the circle of people most important to her, had all made a point of showing up to support her. "I'd like to welcome you to the grand opening of Em+Power Creative.

Please come in."

A cheer rose up as she unlocked the door.

"Wait," Sterling said. "Let me." He swept her up into his arms.

"Sterling, what are you doing?" she squealed.

"What does it look like? I'm carrying you over the threshold."

She smacked him lightly on the shoulder. "It's a business, you goof."

He looked down at her, eyes filled with amusement. "It's still good luck." He stepped through the door into her office and gently set her down, looking around. "Completely you."

She warmed at his praise. In the end, Sterling and her brothers had convinced her to keep the condo in Kansas City and rent it out. She'd been able to use her savings to put a down payment on the live-work space next door to Emmaline's Dress Shop. The second she'd walked in with the real-estate agent, she'd fallen in love with the high ceilings and big windows. Even though it was small, it had an airiness about it that would be perfect for inspiring creativity. She'd brought favorite pieces from her condo, including the enormous farm table to use as meeting and workspace.

"Breakfast is served," Luci called from the table.

The bell on the door jingled, and in walked Sterling's parents, Julie and John, carrying an enormous plant. "Are we too late?" Julie asked.

Emma wrapped the woman in a hug. "Not at all. Welcome. I'm thrilled you made it." True to his word, Sterling had brought her to his parents' house for breakfast the day after the Main Street opening and nighttime fundraiser, and the women had become fast friends. Emma hadn't realized how much she'd missed a mother's touch until Julie had enveloped her in a warm embrace the first time they'd met. Since then, Julie had insisted Emma come for weekly meals.

Brodie raised his coffee cup. "To the best little sister we brothers could have. You've always marched to your own drummer, and we couldn't be more proud of you."

Sterling laced his fingers through hers and raised his cup too. "To new beginnings." His eyes grew soft. "In business and in life." Pressing a kiss to her temple, he murmured low so only she could hear. "I love you, Em."

December

TIRES CRUNCHED OVER the gravel as the car slowed and Sterling cut the engine. The view was just as he remembered – tall evergreens scattered among the gravestones, overlooking the bay. At least it wasn't raining today, although the gray covered them like a blanket. Gray water reflecting silvery clouds.

One year.

One year since they'd buried Johnny. There were still days when the grief sliced through him with a swiftness and intensity that stole his breath. Still days when a random comment from a stranger, or the late afternoon light streaming through the trees triggered a memory that tightened his throat.

Emma covered his hand with hers. "It's a beautiful spot," she said quietly. "So peaceful."

He nodded. "Yeah. I feel like if you're gonna have a view for eternity, this one doesn't suck."

She huffed out a quiet laugh. "You should take a picture and frame it. That way, when you miss Johnny, you can look at it and share the view."

He turned in his seat. "This is why I love you."

She winked at him and flashed him a smile. "I am brilliant, aren't I?" She turned serious, squeezing his hand. "Do you need some time alone? I can wait here in the car. Or go for a walk."

A weight pressed on his chest. So heavy, it closed his throat. He swallowed and took a belly breath. But even that didn't push the feeling away. Twisting his hand so that he could hold Emma's, he brought her knuckles to his lips and pressed a kiss on her soft skin, catching a whiff of her scented lotion. "Come with me?"

"Are you sure?" Concern laced her voice.

"I'm sure." He needed her there with him. And not just for support. "Let's go." He stepped out of the car, grabbing a bag from the back seat and double checking his pocket for the small box as he rounded the front to open Emma's door. She took his hand, and he led her partway down the hill to a gray granite headstone. *Johnson Patrick McCaslin.*

The weight on his chest returned. It was one thing to intellectualize death. To know that someone was gone, to not be able to call or text. To miss the sound of their voice. Their laugh. But the cold stark reality of the headstone was another thing entirely. His knees nearly buckled from the force of it.

Emma's arm slipped around his waist. As if she could sense the intensity of the ache that consumed his body. "I'm so sorry, Sterling."

He could hear the tears in her voice, and he clung to her, letting the sound of the wind in the trees wash over him. Carry away some of his grief. They could have stood there an hour for all he knew, but at some point, the ache eased, and he felt like he could breathe again. Taking a shuddering breath, he lifted his head. "Johnny, meet Emma. Emma," he gestured to the headstone. "Meet Johnny. Best friend, brother-in-arms, trouble causer, rabble rouser." His voice grew tight. "One of the best damn people I've ever known."

Emma pressed a hand to her face, shoulders shaking with quiet tears. "Hi Johnny," she said thickly. "Sterling's told me so much about you. And you have a beautiful family."

When he'd called Macey to let her know he was bringing Emma out and why, she'd insisted they stay with her and Sophie. He clutched the box, heart jumping out of his chest. "I wanted to bring you here not just to meet Johnny. A year ago, I said love is weak. You taught me to be fearless. Emma, your spirit, your fire… has pushed me through my darkest moments. Even when I was a cadet. You've always made me a better person. I love you. And I meant what I said last spring. I want to be your man. Your only. The one who is there for you, pushing you, holding you up. Loving all of you." He pulled his hand from his pocket and dropped to a knee. Emma's eyes jumped wide and she gasped. "Please say you'll be my wife. My forever."

"Yes, yes, yes. Of course, *YES.*" Her voice rose higher with each word and laughter bubbled out of her, even as tears streamed from her eyes. He opened the box and her mouth dropped open. "My God, that's gorgeous."

"Will you wear it?" She nodded vigorously, smiling from ear to ear. "I want you to know, I talked to your brothers–"

"*They knew about this?*" She squealed.

"Oh hon, everyone knew about this." He slipped the ring over her finger. "One of the diamonds was in your mother's engagement ring. The other was in my mom's." His chest grew tight again as he tripped over the words. "And the center stone is the one Johnny gave Macey."

"Oh, Sterling." She squeezed her eyes shut pressing her hand to her chest. "I don't know what to say."

"It was her idea. I never would have asked. But when I told her I wanted to bring you here to propose, she insisted. Said Johnny would love it." He pulled in a breath. "See, Jason and I helped Johnny propose to Macey, helped him pick her ring. Macey said she wanted to keep it in the family."

Emma pulled him up and burrowed into his arms. "I would be honored to wear it."

He cleared his throat. "I have one more thing for you."

Her eyes twinkled up at him. "An engagement present?"

He lifted a shoulder. "Sure. You can call it that." He passed her the bag.

She flicked a glance at the headstone. "You in on this too, Johnny?"

Sterling let his head fall back in a laugh. "Nope. This one was all me." He knew she'd like this one.

She slipped off the bow, and slid a finger under the tape, unwrapping it carefully. Her face registered surprise, then wonder. "When did you get this?"

"At the antique shop the same day you picked up the *Never, never, never give up* artwork."

"But–"

"Just like the picture says–" His chest grew warm with the admission. "I have always known it was you."

She cupped his face and pulled him in for a kiss. "I love you Sterling Walker, with all my heart."

Her lips were like an absolution. A healing balm that filled the holes in his heart. A promise of beauty and spring and everlasting love. He deepened the kiss, losing himself in her.

When they broke apart, her smile parted the clouds, and

the sun burst through in a golden beam. "I have always known it was you, too."

THE BEGINNING OF HAPPILY EVER AFTER

Did you like this book? Please leave a review! Independent authors rely on reviews and word of mouth. If you enjoyed this book, please spread the word!

Want more?

A HERO'S HAVEN – Cash Aiken & Kaycee Starr
(Coming Feb 27th)

A HERO'S HOME – Jason Case & Millie Prescott
(Coming 2018)

A HERO'S HOPE – Braden McCall & Luci Cruz
(Coming 2018)

A HERO'S HAVEN (preorder your copy now!)

Former Navy SEAL Cash Aiken assumed he could leave behind the trauma of war and settle into life as a bodyguard. Why not? He was big, smart, and nothing ever got past his eagle eye. But a split second of inattention nearly cost the life of his asset, and cost him his job. When his old buddy Travis Kincaid invites him to come work at Resolution Ranch, an organization helping wounded vets, he clings to the lifeline and hopes it's a chance to start over. But Cash is stunned to discover that the beautiful woman he nearly let die is hiding out at the ranch, masquerading as a stable hand.

Country Music's Superdiva, Kaycee Starr, is done with the music biz. After a terrifying encounter with a crazed fan, she goes underground and answers a help-wanted ad in a place the paparazzi would never think to look. Prairie, Kansas. While she finds solace and healing among the horses, handsome ranch hand Cash Aiken lights her up in ways she only wrote about in songs. He's the only person she's met who seems to 'get' her.

Cash and Kaycee fall hard and fast for each other, but when their secrets are exposed, will they have the courage to trust each other? And more importantly, themselves?

WHERE IT ALL BEGAN:
THE COWBOYS OF THE FLINT HILLS SERIES

PRAIRIE HEAT – Blake Sinclaire & Maddie Hansen
(on sale now!)

PRAIRIE PASSION – Brodie Sinclaire & Jamey O'Neill
(on sale now!)

PRAIRIE DESIRE – Ben Sinclaire & Hope Hansen
(on sale now!)

PRAIRIE STORM – Axel Hansen & Haley Cooper
(on sale now!)

PRAIRIE FIRE – Parker Hansen & Cassidy Grace
(on sale now!)

PRAIRIE DEVIL – Colton Kincaid & Lydia Grace
(coming in 2018)

PRAIRIE FEVER – Gunnar Hansen & Suzannah Winslow
(coming in 2018)

PRAIRIE BLISS – Jarrod O'Neill & Lexi Grace

PRAIRIE REDEMPTION – Cody Hansen & Carolina Grace

COMING IN APRIL 2018 – PRAIRIE DEVIL

He's the Devil she shouldn't want

Colton Kincaid has a chip on his shoulder. Thrown out of the house when he was seventeen by his brother, Travis, he scrapped his way to the top of the rodeo circuit riding broncs, and never looked back. Until a chance encounter with hometown good girl Lydia Grace leaves him questioning everything and wanting a shot at redemption.

She's the Angel he can never have

All Lydia Grace needs is one break. After having her concepts stolen by a famous shoe designer, she returns home to Prairie to start a boot company on her own. But when her break comes in the form of Colton Kincaid, Prairie's homegrown bad boy and rodeo star, she wonders if she's gotten more than she's bargained for.

They say be careful what you wish for

To get her boot company off the ground, Lydia makes Colton an offer too good to refuse, but he ups the ante. Will the bargain she strikes bring her everything she's dreamed of and more, or did she just make a deal with the devil?

Help a Hero – Read a Cowboy
KISS ME COWBOY – A Box Set for Veterans
Six Western Romance authors have joined up to support their favorite charity – Heroes & Horses – and offer you this sexy box set with Six Full Length Cowboy Novels, filled with steamy kisses and HEA's. Grab your copy and help an American Hero today!

Subscribe to my Newsletter for updates and release information for Prairie Storm and the rest of the Cowboys of the Flint Hills Series.
http://tessalayne.com/newsletter

Join my reader group on Facebook – The Prairie Posse this is where I post my sneak peeks, offer giveaways, and share hot cowboy pics!
facebook.com/groups/1390521967655100

ACKNOWLEDGEMENTS

Twenty-two veterans kill themselves every day. **2-2** Think about that. These are the men and women who place their bodies, *their very lives*, in harms way. That even one veteran feels so hopeless as to take his or her own life is a travesty. It is too many. Countless other veterans sink into despair and end up homeless or unable to function as productive members of society. We can do better. We *must* do better.

To everyone at the organization Heroes & Horses. You inspire me on a daily basis.

To Jinx Kimmer, you're a lifesaver and I'm so grateful for your insights.

To Genevieve Turner, Kara, and Jenny, your willingness to tell it like it is – both the beautiful and the not-so-beautiful have helped make these books shine. Thanks for all you do!

To my fabulous designer, Amanda Kelsey, these covers make my heart sing!

To my mentor Kimberley Troutte, thank you so much for the hand-holding, words of encouragement, and for helping me make sure each book gets it right.

To Erin, thank you so much for all the things! ☺

To Mr. Cowboy, Teenager and Tiny, I treasure each day with you. Words aren't big enough or descriptive enough to convey how much I love you.

Lastly, to my readers in the Prairie Posse. You are an incredible group of women and I'm grateful to spend time with you almost every day. I'm especially grateful for the days when you send virtual supplies of chocolate, wine, and hawt cowboys :D

Made in the USA
San Bernardino, CA
19 June 2020

73807092R00156